A KIDNAPPING IN KENTUCKY 1776

Elizabeth Raum

CHICKEN SCRATCH BOOKS

WWW.CHICKENSCRATCHBOOKS.COM

Chicken Scratch Books
PO Box 104
Wisdom, MT 59761
www.chickenscratchbooks.com

Publisher's Note: This is a work of fiction. Names, characters, places,
and incidents are a product of the author's imagination. Locales and
public names are sometimes used for atmospheric purposes. Any re-
semblance to actual people, living or dead, or to businesses, companies,
events, institutions, or locales is completely coincidental.
Ordering Information: Special discounts are available on quantity
purchases by corporations, associations, and others. For details,
contact the publisher at the address above.

First Chicken Scratch Books Printing, 2022
ISBN 978-1-953743-14-5 (paperback)
ISBN 978-1-953743-15-2 (ebook)

Printed in the United States of America

"America was not built on fear.
America was built on courage,
on imagination, and an unbeatable
determination to do the job at hand."
– Harry S. Truman, U.S. President
1945–1953

THE FIRST DAY
Sunday, July 14, 1776
Mid-afternoon

JOHN GASS'S STORY

I t isn't fair," John mumbled as he slid down the bank into the Kentucky River. He clenched his fist and punched the water. Big droplets splashed into the air.

I'm almost as old as they are. Almost . . . .

But the frontiersmen at the fort treated him as if he was one of the little boys scrambling onto tree stumps and jumping off.

"Come play with us," one of them called.

"Not this time," John said. At twelve, he was too old for childish games.

Then again, he wasn't old enough to be considered a man, either.

Four of the frontiersmen, who had come to Boonesborough to help build the fort, had gone for a hike in the

1

woods. They'd invited his cousin, Big John Gass, to join them. Big John was fifteen. The others were just a bit older. John had wanted to go, too, but they didn't include him. Worse yet, they called him "Little John." He was only three years younger. He was shorter, too, although his britches no longer reached all the way to his ankles. "You're growing like a weed," his mother said. "Soon you'll tower over me."

It couldn't happen soon enough.

John was as brave as any boy who ever lived on the Kentucky frontier—or so he kept telling himself. He could handle a rifle as well as any man. He'd never gotten lost in the vast wilderness of Kentucky. He doubted he ever would. Someday he hoped to be as expert at hunting and tracking as Daniel Boone, who was the best in the entire world.

If only I was a few years older. . . .

He punched the water again and again. Fish scattered. John watched the sunlight glint off the silvery fins of catfish, bluegills, and bass.

Golly! So many fish!

Could he catch one in his hands? John doubted any of the young frontiersmen had ever done it. His cousin hadn't either.

I'll do it! That'll show 'em. Even Daniel Boone will be impressed.

John stood knee-deep in river water. He waited, keeping as still as a fence post. The mud settled, and so did the fish. He felt the tickle of bluegills, who were about the size of his hand, and the longer, sleeker walleyes gliding around his legs. They seemed to think he was just another river rock.

John had been hunting with his father since he was four years old. The first lesson his dad taught him was patience. "Wait and watch," his father said, and that was exactly what John did as fish fluttered against his legs.

Several younger boys stood on the bank above him.

"Whatcha doing?" one called, but John didn't answer. To do so would scare the fish away.

John bent down, hands poised to grab a fish.

Slowly,

slowly,

slowly. . . .

Splash!

A rock landed by John's feet, and the fish scattered.

He turned toward the bank, fists clenched, anger in his eyes.

"I wasn't trying to hit you," Danny Boone yelled.

John sighed and turned away. Danny was six. How could he know that John was trying to catch a fish? Tossing rocks into the river was something the little boys did for fun.

John climbed out of the water and trudged up the bank. If only there was another boy his age at the fort.

Or if I was a few years older. . . .

John's father, Captain David Gass, had brought the family to Boonesborough last September. They'd joined Daniel Boone and his family on the trek from North Carolina. They'd crossed the Cumberland Gap and followed Boone's Trace all the way to Kentucky. The trip of over 300 miles had taken more than three weeks.

Seventeen young frontiersmen joined the group to build the fort and keep the settlers safe. Even so, the fort wasn't finished. Building a fort was hard work; hunting and hiking through the wilderness proved more fun. Oh, the frontiersmen stood guard when women and children worked in the gardens or fetched the cows from the woods, but finishing the fort? They hadn't bothered. At least there hadn't been any Indian attacks on the fort. Not yet.

Other settlements had been attacked. So had isolated cabins. John's mother lived in fear of an attack. But John wasn't worried. He rubbed the handle of the knife in his belt. He knew how to use it.

I can take care of myself—and my mother, too.

He glanced up to see Jemima Boone limping toward him. "Good day, Jemima!"

"Good day, John."

Jemima was a year older than John, but she didn't look down on him like the older boys did. She was wearing her best dress with a flouncy petticoat underneath, an apron on top, and a bonnet to protect her from the July sunshine. A few strands of long dark hair escaped the bonnet.

"What happened?" he asked, pointing to her gimpy foot. She was barefoot, as usual.

"Cane-stab," she said.

John grimaced. He'd stepped on the sharp bits of cane growing in patches along the river's edge, too. It was like stepping on the needles Mother used for sewing.

"It happened yesterday when I was fetching the cows," Jemima said. "It pains me something terrible."

John nodded sympathetically but said nothing.

Jemima hobbled away.

John sighed as he watched her.

Golly! I wish I could have said something helpful.

After all, Jemima was a friend. On the long journey from North Carolina to Kentucky, they herded cows together along the rough-cut trail. There was little need for conversation, which suited John perfectly. He was all about action, not talk.

He spun a rock across the river. It skipped four times: a record. But it was too late; no one was watching. A cornfield now stood between him and Jemima, and the little boys had scattered.

Would he be caught in-between forever—too young to be of value and too old to be mollycoddled?

It wasn't that he wanted to be pampered, but it would be nice to be noticed from time to time.

THE FIRST DAY
Sunday, July 14, 1776
Mid-afternoon

JEMIMA BOONE'S STORY

Three-year-old Jesse tugged on Jemima's skirt. She sighed and smiled down at him, knowing that he needed something, and she'd be the one to do it. There was always work to do. Watching the younger children was one of Jemima's many chores. She loved Jesse, but oh, how she wanted a few hours to spend with her friends. Family was fine, but they always needed something. What Jemima needed was simply a bit of time of her own.

"Duck?" Jesse said again. He called her "Duck." So did the rest of her brothers and sisters. Jemima loved the water. "You swim like a duck," her Daddy once said, and it became a family nickname, which made the children laugh. Jemima didn't mind, so long as it stayed in the

7

family.

But if anyone else starts calling me "Duck," they'll find themselves head-to-head with a bear, a bear named Jemima.

"What do you need, Jesse?" she asked.

"Danny promised to play wif me," Jesse said, and he looked so forlorn that Jemima simply had to help. "He's most likely down by the river." She set the broom aside. "Come along then. We'll find him."

Jemima limped along with Jesse in tow. It wasn't far to the river. The fort sat adjacent to it, and the Boone's cabin wasn't far away. The area was littered with tree stumps where the men had cut logs to build the fort. They'd also cleared a section for crops. The corn grew tall in the rich soil, and the ears were nearly ripe.

Danny was playing with the other small boys. They made play guns from strong, hollow cane stalks and took turns pretending to be hunter or deer. Jesse ran to Danny, and the others let him join the game.

He'll probably end up being the deer.

But there was no harm in the game. One day they'd be hunting real deer with real guns. For now, it was just pretend.

Jemima noticed her younger sisters picking dandelions at the river's edge. Her mother used the bright flowers to dye yarn yellow.

John Gass stood nearby. He was soaking wet.

"Been swimming, John?"

"Not on purpose," he said.

"Oh, fell in?"

"Fishing," he said.

Jemima smiled. John was always involved in some adventure. She and John had been friends forever. After her family's first unsuccessful attempt to reach Boonesborough, Captain Gass had offered the Boones a place to stay on his own property in North Carolina. Captain Gass was a loyal friend to Daniel Boone, and when the Boones decided to make a second try to reach Kentucky, the Gass family joined them.

Jemima exchanged only a few words with John before she noticed the fort's dugout canoe tied to a nearby tree. She forgot all about John, and she forgot, at least for a moment, the pain in her foot. Her vision narrowed until all she saw was the canoe inviting her for a ride on the river.

Well, not exactly 'inviting,' but no one else needed it, and soaking her foot in the cool river would ease her pain. She would sit back in the dugout and let her foot dangle in the water.

Yes, it is exactly what I need—not just relief from pain, but a real adventure.

Once she was floating down the river, she'd be free—free from the endless chores, free from constant supervision, free to have fun with friends.

She stumbled toward her family's cabin without even saying "good-bye" to John. She wanted to talk to her father before he settled in for his Sunday afternoon nap. If her foot hadn't been so sore, she would have run. As it was, she limped along as fast as she could.

Everyone at the fort worked hard all week. But Sunday was a day of rest. That morning, everyone had gathered beneath the ancient elm tree at the river's edge for Bible reading. They dressed in their best clothes as if they were going to a real church. But there was no church at Boonesborough. There wasn't a school or a store or much of anything except the half-built fort and a few cabins scattered around the periphery. Sunday afternoon was free time for most everyone.

With the canoe, she could grab some freedom for herself.

Most of the cabins stood inside the fort, forming the walls. "It's safer that way," the settlers said. But Daniel Boone built his outside the walls, a short distance from the fort.

Jemima smiled as the cabin came into view. It was a good, cozy home. When the Boones had first arrived at Boonesborough, they lived in a log hut in the hollow, but as soon as he could, her dad built this sturdier house with wooden floors and a strong door. He'd even put glass panes in the windows. The fireplace kept them warm on rainy winter nights. So did the buffalo furs that served as both mattresses and blankets.

Daniel Boone stood outside the cabin talking to Nathan Reid. Reid was a skilled hunter. He'd arrived in Boonesborough with his friend John Floyd, one of the men who had joined the party to guard the settlers. Both men were eager to claim a piece of Kentucky for themselves.

Jemima waited patiently until the men stopped talking.

"What do you need, Lass?" her father asked.

"It's a perfect day for a canoe ride on the river."

Daniel Boone smiled and shook his head. "Aye, so it is. Would you be asking for yourself and the Callaway girls?"

Jemima nodded. "Please, Daddy."

Daniel looked from Jemima to Nathan. "Perhaps if someone were to go along to keep you company. . . ."

Jemima followed her father's gaze.

"I'd be happy to go," Nathan said.

"Then it's settled. You're a good man, Nathan Reid."

They all knew it wasn't company Reid would provide; it was safety.

Daniel turned to Jemima. "Be watchful and avoid the northern bank. The Shawnee villages are to the north. If there are Shawnee hunters in the area, they'll favor that side of the river."

"We'll be careful, I promise. Thank you, Daddy."

Daniel Boone entered the cabin to strip off his shirt, kick his moccasins aside, and settle in for a long nap as he did every Sunday.

Jemima hurried to the fort to find Fanny and Betsy.

On Sunday afternoons, women gathered to visit, children played, and the frontiersmen practiced shooting, held wrestling matches, or set out on hikes through the countryside. The young men loved spending time in the great Kentucky outdoors as much as Daniel Boone did. Jemima loved the wilderness, too, but her father had forbidden her to wander free.

But now, Jemima's spirits soared. After months of peace, he had agreed to let her take the canoe for a cruise on the river. She was certain that the Callaway girls would be eager to go along.

The Callaway's cabin formed part of one wall. Betsy Callaway was sixteen; her sister Fanny was fourteen, just a few months older than Jemima.

Jemima hadn't even finished asking when they cried, "Oh, yes. We'd love to go."

"Let us have an adventure," Fanny said, which made Jemima smile. She was thinking the exact same thing. Like Jemima, Fanny and Betsy were sick and tired of being safe. It wasn't that they wanted to court danger, it was just that they had been stuck in their cabins or restricted to the half-built fort for months. They called it being "forted," and it was no fun, no fun at all. The cabins got stuffy, and the fort had begun to feel like a prison. They had hoped that spring would bring freedom. It hadn't. The young men were allowed to wander into the woods, but not the girls.

They knew their parents were simply trying to protect them from a possible Indian attack, but, oh, it seemed so unfair, especially when they had to stay inside. And if they went out to plant the garden or fetch the cows, a guard went along with his rifle ready.

"The forest is dangerous," their parents said. "Wolves, bears, and . . . hunters. If you are caught alone in the woods. . . ." They didn't need to finish the sentence.

Jemima knew that it wasn't only animals that posed a threat. Her dad told her that Kentucky was called "the bloody ground," and it wasn't just because Indian hunters killed animals there. Sometimes they attacked settlers. Sometimes they even fought one another.

And as if Indian attack wasn't bad enough, Jemima had overheard her father say that a war between the American colonies and Great Britain was likely. "A revolution," he said.

"If so," one of the men said, "the British are likely to convince the tribes to side with them."

"Tis likely," agreed another.

But for the time being, at least, all was peaceful. There hadn't been any Indian sightings in months. Oh, a few Indian hunters had probably passed by unnoticed, but none had stopped at the fort or threatened the settlers.

A canoe ride on the river would be perfectly safe. Wouldn't it?

THE FIRST DAY
Sunday, July 14, 1776
Later that Afternoon

JOHN'S STORY

After Jemima left and the younger boys wandered off, John slipped back down the riverbank into the shallow water for another try at catching a fish barehanded. He was a never-give-up kind of boy. "I can do this," he said aloud. "If anyone can, I can."

It couldn't be that hard, could it?

He waited for the river mud, which had bubbled around his feet, to settle. He dipped his hand into the water. The fish scattered and disappeared, but that didn't matter. They weren't the ones he planned to catch. He bent down and felt along the river bottom. Somewhere, among the rocks, he'd find a catfish nest, and when he did, he'd reach in and grab the sucker. It would bite, but that was a small price to pay. Catfish have lots of teeth, but they aren't very sharp. John wasn't going to let a little pain stop him. He'd wrestle that catfish out of the water and carry it home to his mother in triumph. He grinned as he imagined her smile. His dad would be proud too, and his older brothers would be amazed that he pulled off such a feat.

But when he bent down to search beneath the rocks, something big butted him from behind.

SPLASH!

John toppled facedown into the river. He came up gurgling and spitting water. "Golly, Ranger!"

The big dog splashed in the water and licked John's face.

"I suppose I can't be mad at you," John said. Ranger was a good dog. He didn't mean to spoil a brilliant plan any more than the little boys had earlier.

The girls picking dandelions giggled as John climbed out of the water dripping wet. When Ranger showered them with water, they giggled some more. John couldn't help but smile . . . until he noticed Jemima and the Callaway girls standing nearby.

"You look a sight," Jemima said, and she burst out laughing. "How's the water?"

John brushed a hand through his wet hair trying to make himself presentable. Water dripped down his face. "It felt fine." He tried to act as if an afternoon swim had been his plan all along.

"We'll soon find out for ourselves, although we plan to stay dry. We're taking the canoe out on the river," Jemima said.

John raised his eyebrows.

"My father gave his blessing," she said. "And Nathan Reid said he'd come with us."

If Daniel Boone said it was fine, who was he to disagree? But John couldn't help worrying.

It doesn't seem like a good idea to me.

For months women and children had been told to stay near the fort. It was no secret that the tribes who hunted in the area considered the settlers invaders. There had been attacks on other settlements. Boonesborough might be next. It wasn't just his mother who was worried; Daddy was, too.

The canoe was tied to a small tree several feet away. John watched the girls slide down the bank and step into the dugout. He had no idea how they did it without getting their dresses wet. The girls' dresses reached nearly to the ground with layers of flouncy petticoats beneath. John was glad he didn't have to wear such troublesome togs.

The little girls picking wildflowers along the riverbank asked, "Can we go?"

"Yes. Let us go, too," Jemima's younger sisters cried.

Cuzzy Callaway pleaded with her big sisters. "Please!"

"Not this time," Betsy said, and even though the younger ones kept begging to go along, the answer remained a very firm "no."

"I thought Nathan Reid was coming," John said. Having a guard along seemed like a wise idea.

Everyone looked toward the fort. There was no sign of Nathan.

"Must we wait?" Betsy asked.

John listened as the girls talked it over. "It's getting late," Fanny said. "Mother will be expecting us home to help with supper."

"We'd best be off," Betsy said, and so they climbed into the canoe.

John looked up and down the river. He shifted from foot to foot.

The girls on the river alone? It's just not right.

He looked toward the fort, hoping Nathan would appear before the girls left. John was tempted to ask Jemima if he could go. He'd keep the girls safe and make Captain Boone proud, but their quick refusal when the little girls asked, stopped him. It was bad enough that the older boys didn't want him along. It would be even worse if the girls turned him down, too.

"Can you give us a hand, John?" Jemima called.

Was she going to ask him to go along?

His hope was dashed an instant later when Jemima said, "Untie the dugout and give us a push."

John did as she asked. He untied the tug and tossed it to Jemima. And then he gave the canoe a mighty shove.

The Callaway sisters sat up front and paddled into the middle of the river. Jemima sat behind them, her sore foot trailing out the back of the canoe.

John watched until the dugout canoe disappeared around the bend in the river.

THE FIRST DAY
Sunday, July 14, 1776
On the River

JEMIMA'S STORY

Free at last," Jemima said, as the dugout drifted further from shore. She lay back and dangled her sore foot in the water. The river formed a deep pool near the fort, and Jemima looked over the side and watched the fish swimming below.

Sun sparkled on the water; a breeze rippled it. Jemima's dad loved the wilderness—the beauty of it, the solitude—and so did Jemima.

Long before they moved to Kentucky, her father told her about the trails winding through the forest, trails made by vast herds of buffalo and elk. He told of beaver dams dotting the ponds, of silvery fish in the Kentucky River, and of birds overhead so thick they blocked the sun. "North Carolina is getting too crowded.

I need elbow room," he said. It was a feeling Jemima understood.

As the canoe traveled further from the confining fort, Jemima sighed. "Free at last," she said again as she swished her hand through the warm river water.

But she couldn't ignore the dangers of frontier life. Her daddy didn't. He told of panthers and wildcats that prowled the wilderness. At night, wolves howled. By day, bears roamed the forest paths. So did Indian warriors.

Two years earlier, the Boones had attempted to reach Boonesborough. Her older brother James had gone for supplies, and when he was returning to the camp, he'd been killed by Indians. Heartsick, the Boones returned to North Carolina. Captain Gass offered them a place to stay until they were ready to try again for Kentucky. Her mother and father seldom spoke of James, but she knew they missed him as much as she did.

They needed time to heal, and within a year Jemima's mother, Rebecca, was expecting another baby, her ninth. She wasn't fit to travel, so they waited until the baby was born. It had been a difficult birth. Baby William died a few days later, and Rebecca didn't feel well enough to travel for several weeks.

Even so, Kentucky kept calling.

In September 1775, they left North Carolina for the second time. Her dad recruited several young frontiersmen to act as guards, and there had been no more attacks.

The Boones settled into life in the wilderness, hoping to live in harmony with the Indians. After all, the old chiefs had signed a treaty giving the land to Colonel Richard Henderson and his Transylvania Company. The Boones were there with Henderson's blessing to build the fort and establish a settlement.

There were no Indian towns or villages in Kentucky. Instead, it was a hunting ground, not just for the Shawnee, but for many tribes who depended on Kentucky's plentiful wildlife for food, blankets, and other necessities of life. Daniel Boone was a hunter, too, and friend to many Indians. He admired their skills, and so did Jemima.

The canoe glided past rocky cliffs studded with towering trees, past 15-foot-high patches of cane growing at the river's edge, and past clumps of colorful wildflowers. Jemima dipped her hands into the cool water. The river was not as deep here; she could see pebbles along the bottom.

She gabbed and gossiped and giggled with Fanny and Betsy, who guided the canoe. The girls had their pick of eligible young frontiersmen. There were nearly twenty at the fort. Betsy was engaged to Sam Henderson. Jemima was sweet on a Callaway cousin named Flanders, and Fanny liked John Holder. Fanny and Jemima were too young to marry but not too young to dream.

"Look! Columbine!" Fanny pointed to the delicate lavender flowers dotting the shore. "Shall we stop and pick them?"

Jemima hesitated. "Daddy said we should stay away from the north shore."

"And you always obey him?" Fanny teased. She knew that Jemima had caused more than her share of mischief.

"The flowers are pretty," Jemima agreed. The delicate Columbine would brighten up the cabin, which tended to be dark. The windows were small and didn't allow much light to filter through. Candlelight was dim, and even a roaring fire didn't light the corners. But she didn't change her mind. "We should stay far from the shore."

Fanny and Betsy teased her a bit. "Are you afeared?"

Jemima simply shook her head and leaned back. She wasn't really afraid; it was simply that she tried to do what her father said. She didn't always succeed, it was true, but if he found out, he'd be disappointed, and one thing Jemima hated was to disappoint her daddy.

"I shouldn't have teased you. If anybody in Boones-borough has courage, you do," Fanny said, which made Jemima smile.

"My mother always says, 'Be strong.' So, I try," Jemima said.

"Your mother is like my grandmother," Betsy said. "She told me that the words, 'Be Not Afraid,' are in the Holy Bible sixty-three times. She actually counted."

"Imagine Grandmother doing that," Fanny said. Both girls smiled at the memory.

"I suppose we have to be strong living so far from towns and cities," Betsy said. She looked wistfully into the sky. "Sometimes I wish . . . ."

She didn't need to finish the thought. They were all aware that that life on the frontier was hard. There were so many dangers lurking in the thick Kentucky forests.

But when Betsy and Fanny tried to paddle away from the shore, a strong current grabbed the dugout and pulled it toward a sandbar. With the water mid-summer low, there were lots of sandbars along the way. This one seemed particularly vicious. It grabbed the dugout and wouldn't let it go.

Betsy and Fanny struggled with the oars, pushing first on one side and then on the other. The boat rocked back and forth, and Jemima grabbed the side of the canoe to steady herself.

"It won't move," Fanny said.

The girls pushed against the sandbar with their paddles. Jemima sat up straight and helped rock the boat back and forth.

They heard a splash and saw a man lunge into the water. He grabbed the rope at the front of the canoe.

Jemima sat up. "What . . . ?"

But before she could finish the sentence, Fanny yelled, "Law! Simon! How you scared me."

Jemima lay back. Simon was one of the Callaway's servants.

"That's not Simon," Betsy shrieked. "It's an Indian!"

Fanny had mistaken the black war paint on the face of a Cherokee brave for Simon's dark skin.

"Yell!" Jemima said, and she began screaming. "Halloo! Help! Halloo!" She looked toward the fort, which was hidden behind the bend in the river. They hadn't gone far, but they were out of sight. Were they out of hearing range?

"We have to get help," Jemima shouted, and she screamed even louder, praying that someone—anyone— would hear her calls for help and come to the rescue.

For a few seconds, Betsy was paralyzed, unable to move. Not Fanny. She grabbed her paddle and hit the man over the head.

THWACK!

THWACK!

THWACK!

. . . until the paddle broke in half and Fanny stumbled backward, landing on top of Jemima.

Jemima pushed Fanny away and struggled to stand up. But her foot was half in and half out of the canoe, so she kept losing her balance, and falling back into the dugout. She didn't stop calling for help.

Betsy grabbed the other paddle and swatted the man.

THWACK!

He brushed her away as if she were no more than a bothersome mosquito.

The boat rocked so precariously that Fanny, who was standing, grabbed an edge of the dugout and held on lest she fall overboard. Both of the Callaway girls commenced to screaming for help. Betsy kept waving the broken paddle at the attacker.

The canoe rocked back and forth as the girls struggled to push it off the sandbar and away from the Indian. It tipped this way and that. It threatened to overturn and then . . . .

Four more men burst out of the cane.

The girls shrieked. They might have been able to defeat one man, but five . . . .

The men flashed knives and tomahawks.

The girls screamed even louder.

And then one of the men seized a fistful of Betsy's hair, pulled it back, and raised his tomahawk above her head. The threat was clear. Be still or else . . . .

The girls quieted mid-scream.

The man let go of Betsy's hair.

Jemima was glad her own hair was held in place with several combs and hidden beneath her bonnet. Otherwise, it would cascade down her back and reach nearly to her knees.

"Be strong," Jemima whispered, praying the Callaway girls would hear. "We have to be strong."

Two of the men pulled the dugout to shore and signaled the girls to get out.

Betsy went first.

Fanny followed.

It took Jemima a bit longer to climb out of the canoe and onto the narrow sandbar that formed the shore. A steep cliff rose directly from the river. Small bushes grew out of rock crevices in the cliff.

The men pulled the boat ashore and ordered the girls to be still, and then one of the men shoved the canoe back into the river.

The girls didn't say a word as they watched the canoe float away. They didn't dare yell. They didn't even dare whisper, but they did exchange worried looks. Betsy shrugged as if to say, "We don't have a choice."

Fanny nodded.

Jemima looked from one to the other, closed her

eyes, and hung her head.

We've been captured!

Jemima reached out and grabbed a small branch overhanging the river, trying to steady the thoughts racing through her head.

A plan. I need a plan.

As the men pushed and pulled the girls up the steep cliff rising from the river's edge, Jemima struggled to focus.

Stay calm. Think!

The men spoke to one another in Shawnee and Cherokee. Jemima understood a few words of the Shawnee language, more than she was willing to let on, and some messages were clear enough without words. A raised tomahawk didn't require translation.

"Faster," one of the men said in English. Jemima wasn't surprised. The hunters who had visited the Boone's cabin back in North Carolina spoke a mix of languages.

Jemima studied the men. She had no trouble identifying the tribes to which they belonged. After all, Indian hunters had often stopped by the Boone cabin in North Carolina. Three of the men were Shawnee; two were Cherokee. The Shawnees wore multiple earrings in each ear and silver nose rings. The Cherokees wore just one earring. All five had shaved their heads except for a single scalp lock, and they had painted black marks on their faces and necks. They were lean and well-muscled and wore long, loose-fitting hunting shirts, breechcloths, and leggings.

The man climbing the hill ahead of her wore soft moccasins.

They reminded her of her father. She pictured her dad, dressed in the same manner as these men—long, loose-fitting hunting shirt, breechcloth, and leggings. He even carried the same weapons: tomahawks, knives, and rifles. After years of living in the wilderness, Daniel Boone found Indian ways more practical than those of European hunters. He didn't wear earrings or shave his head, but he had the same lean, muscular build as these men.

Jemima was sure that as soon as he realized she was missing, Daddy would come searching. He'd find her. She was counting on it. For the first time since the attack, she took a deep breath and relaxed.

She had a plan.

When they reached the plateau above the river, Jemima reached for Fanny's hand and bent close enough to whisper one word: "Delay."

Fanny nodded and whispered the same word into Betsy's ear.

THE FIRST DAY
Sunday, July 14, 1776
After the Girls Leave

JOHN'S STORY

John watched Jemima, Fanny, and Betsy paddle off. "It isn't right," he said, still a bit worried about the girls going off alone, and even more distressed that he was stuck at the fort. Everyone else seemed to be having an adventure.

He tossed a stick into the woods. Ranger ran after it. It was a familiar game. When Ranger tired of fetching, John practiced his game of mumbley peg.

He and his cousin often played, and John was determined to get the better of Big John. It was a test of skill. The goal was to flip the knife from the shoulder, the knees, the nose—in front, behind, and sideways—so that it always landed standing straight up in the ground. There was one move that John hadn't mastered: tossing the knife backward over his head.

He tried once, twice, and on the third time . . . he did it!

I knew I could.

If only someone had been there to see. . . .

John pulled the knife out of the ground. A knife and a tomahawk were fine tools, but a rifle was the real prize. Most boys received one on their 13th birthday. John's birthday wouldn't happen for months. It seemed forever. His dearest wish was that he'd get a rifle. John knew how to handle a gun, and when he had one of his own . . .well, at that point, he'd truly be a man.

He took a deep breath and surveyed the nearby forest. A year from now, he'd be bringing home a deer or an elk, one he'd shot with his own rifle. What a day that would be!

"RAT-TAT-TAT."

John spotted the woodpecker in a nearby tree.

"RAT-TAT-TAT."

He saw the flapping wings of hummingbirds and heard the HUM their wings made.

Leaves RUSTLED in the summer breeze, and a pinecone spiraled down and landed with a gentle PLOP near his feet.

Twigs SNAPPED as squirrels and chipmunks scampered across the forest floor. John recognized each

31

of these sounds.

And then he heard something else.

HALLOO! HELP!

From the river.

John ran to the riverbank. He searched, but he couldn't see beyond the point where the river twisted out of sight.

HELP!

Jemima? It had to be.

The little girls picking dandelions heard it, too. They stopped playing and stood still listening.

Three small boys playing in the mud jumped up, wiped their hands on their britches, and listened.

They all heard more screams, frantic ones.

John didn't stop to think; he dashed toward the fort yelling, "It's the gals! They're in trouble! Hurry!"

Several younger children tagged along behind him, but John quickly outdistanced them. He yelled so loud that everyone could hear. "The girls are in trouble!"

Men and women stopped what they were doing and rushed out of the stockade.

"The girls?" Mrs. Callaway asked.

"On the river?" Mrs. Boone asked.

"Yes!" John said. "Didn't you hear them scream-ing?"

Everyone stopped talking and stood absolutely still.

But there were no more screams.

"Maybe it was just a coyote," one man suggested.

"No," John insisted. "It was the girls."

The adults stared at him.

"It was our girls," he said again in his firmest voice.

"I heard it, too," Cuzzy Callaway said, and the other children nodded.

The women turned pale. Some began to cry.

"Lord help us! They've been kidnapped," Mrs. Callaway said. It was the only thing that made sense. The girls could all swim, and they knew how to handle the dugout. What else could it be? She bowed her head in prayer.

The other women wrung their hands. Babies whimpered and clung to their mothers as if they understood what was happening. Toddlers grabbed fistfuls of their mothers' aprons.

Everyone rushed to the river—everyone except John.

He raced on toward the Boone's cabin, which sat a short distance apart. He flung open the door.

"What's all that shouting?" Daniel Boone asked leaping off the bed.

"Jemima, Sir! She's been taken."

Captain Boone grabbed his rifle and raced out the door. He didn't bother to put on a shirt or moccasins, just put on his pantaloons and dashed to the river barefoot. John chased after him.

The settlers were already at the river when Daniel Boone rushed up. John was right behind him. There was no sign of the girls.

Cuzzy Callaway pointed into the distance. "We heard them shouting," she said.

Sam Henderson, who had been shaving when he got the news, dropped his razor and ran to the river with only half his face shaved.

"We'll find 'em," Captain Boone said. "We'll bring 'em home."

"But how?" Sam shouted. "They took the only dugout."

John's dad appeared at his side. "What's the ruckus?" he asked.

"It's Jemima and the Callaway gals," John said. "They've been taken."

Several of the women cried out. "Our poor, poor girls," one moaned.

"Shawnee, I expect. They must have been waiting on the northern shore, and when they saw the girls . . . ." John Floyd said.

"And we've no canoe to go after them," Sam Henderson added, his face twisted in desperation.

It seemed hopeless . . . until John spied the canoe

on the opposite shore. The current had carried it back to Boonesborough. "Look!" he called. "There's the dugout."

It bobbed upside down in the weeds across the river from the fort.

"I see it," someone called. The river was deep. If the men tried to swim across, their gunpowder would be wet and useless.

John studied the river. The current was swift, but he was sure he could manage it.

I'll get it.

And before anyone could stop him, John stripped off his shirt and plunged into the river.

"John's swimming for the dugout!" someone yelled.

Several frontiersmen lined up along the riverbank, rifles in hand.

John risked a glance back at Boonesborough. He saw men aiming their guns at him. He was trying to help. What were they thinking?

He shook his head to clear his thoughts and realized they weren't aiming at him. They were covering him in case he was attacked. If that happened, the riflemen would open fire. Of course, he might become the unintended target. He knew the men were good shots, but so were the Indians.

He brushed those thoughts aside. It was too late to turn back. He'd get the dugout. He had to if they were going to save the girls. Even if he could have turned back, he wouldn't do it.

But it wasn't Indians that worried John. He was a good swimmer, but still . . . a swift river current might sweep him away. He focused on the opposite shore, his muscles tense as he took one stroke after another. Powerful kicks pushed him forward. He struggled to stay on course.

He gritted his teeth and swam on.

Swim.

Swim fast!

One stroke.

Then another.

And another.

A strong kick.

Again.

And again.

The men lining the shore tensed when something RUSTLED in the bushes across the river.

A bird rose from the weeds in flight. They relaxed. So did John.

John listened for the shriek of Indian war cries or the TWANG and WHISTLE of an arrow aimed his way, but all he heard was the SPLASH of fish jumping out of the water into the sun.

To the people watching and worrying, John's swim

across the river seemed to take hours. In truth, it took only minutes.

When John reached the dugout, he flipped it over, grabbed the buffalo tug, and dragged it back toward Fort Boonesborough.

John's mind was racing. River current had sent the canoe back toward the fort, but there was no sign of Jemima. She wasn't in the water, that was obvious.

Jemima was a good swimmer. On the trip over the Wilderness Road, she had forded all the streams without a problem. When they had crossed one turbulent creek, John's four-year-old brother had been swept downstream. It was Jemima who rescued him.

Now, it's my turn to save her.

Several men reached out to help drag the dugout ashore.

Everyone broke into cheers.

"HUZZAH! Hurray for John Gass!"

John dipped his head modestly, in part to hide his smile. For the moment at least, he was a hero. Even the sun smiled down at him.

"Well done, lad," Captain Boone said. "Now we track 'em down."

THE FIRST DAY
Sunday, July 14, 1776
After the Capture

JEMIMA'S STORY

Jemima stood at the edge of the cliff and stared down at the water. The canoe had floated away.

All I wanted was a few minutes of freedom.

And now. . . .

She spied the tall patch of cane where the kidnappers had hidden. It was trampled and bent, which gave Jemima a new idea. *We'll mark the trail! That'll help Daddy find us.*

She was certain the Indians planned on taking them to the Shawnee villages on the Ohio, miles to the north. If the men had wanted to kill them, they could have done that beside the river. But the men made them climb the cliff.

Jemima faced the terrible reality that she was now a

captive, not free, maybe never to be free again.

Had anyone heard her screams?

Jemima thought of John. He was younger than her brother James, of course, but she knew that if John heard them, he would sound the alarm just as James would have done.

Cuzzy and the other little girls must have heard us, too. Someone must have heard.

After a short rest at the top of the cliff, one of the men, the one Fanny had mistaken for Simon, said "move along." It sounded like a growl. He rubbed his head where Fanny had battered him with the oar, narrowed his eyes, and grimaced. He looked as fierce as a bear.

That's what I'll call him. Bear.

Jemima glanced at Fanny and Betsy, hoping they'd understand what she was about to do.

She jutted her chin forward. "I'm not going anywhere," she said. She didn't move; she was willing to chance everything to regain her freedom.

The man she thought of as Bear gave her a gentle shove. "Walk," he said. His voice was harsh, still growly. Jemima wondered if his head hurt. Fanny had pounded him several times.

"I'd rather die than walk barefoot," Jemima said. She pointed to her foot. "Cane-stab."

"Let me see," one of the other men said. He looked

familiar.

There had always been Indians from various tribes visiting the Boone cabin back in North Carolina. He could have been there, but that seemed so long ago. He was older than the others, tall and thin. He carried himself like a king, or at least as Jemima imagined a king might do.

Jemima collapsed onto a nearby rock. The King gently lifted her foot and examined it. "Cane-stab," he said, nodding to the others.

One of the men reached into his pack and handed Jemima a pair of soft moccasins. She gulped at the unexpected kindness. The man was young, not much older than James had been when he was killed.

These men would never do such a dreadful thing. Would they?

Some people called the Indians *savages*, but savages were wild, not kind, and this was an act of kindness. When she accepted the gift, the young Shawnee smiled and nodded in a most gentlemanly way.

Moccasin, that's what I'll call him, not out loud, of course, but in my heart.

She gently pulled a moccasin first onto her sore foot, and then onto the other. Fanny was barefooted, too. Without waiting to be asked, the man gave Fanny a pair of moccasins.

40

Betsy shook her head. She didn't need them. She was wearing the fashionable shoes that her father had bought for her on a recent trip to Virginia. They were leather slippers with wooden heels.

The Callaway girls turned toward Jemima as if she could explain what was happening. She shrugged and held out her hands, unsure what to think. Maybe this was simply a way to hurry them along, but she'd rather consider it a kindness.

On the other hand, these men did kidnap us . . . .

It would definitely be easier walking in the soft leather moccasins than trudging through the wilderness barefoot. There was cane everywhere. And pinecones. And roots coming out of the ground as if to snare anyone on the path. Despite the moccasins, Jemima planned to walk as slowly as possible. She remained sitting on the rock, and no one urged her to move.

Just moments ago, the men had seemed anxious to leave. Now they stared at the girls and spoke to one another in Shawnee. Jemima knew a few words; she might have been able to understand them if they had spoken louder, but their expressions revealed nothing.

At least we aren't moving.

A delay would give her father time to catch up.

All three girls had heard stories of white women taken captive. Such stories were common on the frontier. They knew the story of Mary Rowlandson, who had been taken captive by the Wampanoag a hundred years earlier in Massachusetts. Her book about the experience was famous. She'd been held for eleven weeks before her husband paid a ransom, and the kidnappers let her go. A ransom? Betsy and Fanny's father was rich, but Daniel Boone was lucky if he could scrape up enough cash to buy a bag of flour and a bit of cloth for Rebecca. He wouldn't be able to pay a ransom.

Oh, Daddy, hurry!

Jemima and the Callaway girls would have to use their heads to outwit the kidnappers. Screaming may have been a good start, but it wasn't enough. They'd been about a quarter of a mile from Boonesborough when the Indians captured them. Jemima silently asked the same questions over and over.

Did our screams reach Boonesborough?

Did the trees muffle our voices?

Had the little girls picking flowers heard us?

What about the boys playing by the river?

And John Gass? He's clever. If he heard, he'd have told Daddy.

Suddenly, Fanny leaped sideways. She nearly knocked Betsy over. The kidnappers were kneeling in front of both girls, their knives withdrawn from their belts.

"No!" Fanny shrieked. She staggered to the edge of the cliff. Betsy followed her, and they clung to one another, dread in their eyes. Bits of dirt and loose rocks fell to the river below. One more step back, and they would tumble over the edge. Maybe murder was the plan after all.

Jemima stayed where she was; she didn't dare move. She stared at the men as if that would stop whatever was about to happen, but when she studied their expressions, she realized the men didn't look angry. But they weren't smiling either.

The King stood aside; he didn't stop the others. Bear looked fierce, and even Moccasin, the kind one, had a knife in his hand! Surely, if they were about to kill their captives, their faces would show some emotion. Instead, they looked the way her dad looked when he was cutting logs for the fort or building a fire in the cabin's fireplace. It was as if they had a particular task in mind.

Jemima jumped at the sound of ripping cloth.

One of the Cherokees, whose war paint formed a mask around his eyes, slashed Betsy's dress at the knees. He cut both the dress and the petticoats beneath. And then Mask ripped the fabric into strips.

Another one of the Shawnees, who had a slash of red warpaint on his cheek, chopped off Fanny's skirt at the knees. The men handed the girls the torn strips.

"Wrap your legs," Red Paint said.

The King stepped out of the shadows and approached Jemima. She stood as still as a statue when he cut through her best Sunday dress. She'd sewn it herself from linen her father had bought at the company store in Virginia during one of his trading missions. What a shame to see it ripped apart! There were no stores at Boonesborough. It might be months before she could get more cloth—if ever.

She chided herself for thinking about a dress. After all, a torn dress was the least of her worries. Being separated from her family and carted off to some remote Shawnee village was far worse.

She wrapped the lacy cloth strips up her legs and secured the loose ends to make leggings. Short skirts and leggings would make travel easier in the thick Kentucky forest.

But Jemima had no intention of making anything easy.

She would do whatever she could to cause delays.

THE FIRST DAY
Sunday, July 14, 1776
After Retrieving the Dugout

JOHN'S STORY

John climbed out of the water and hopped from one foot to the other. He was itching to join the search, for there would be a search, of that he was sure, and he didn't want to miss out.

He rushed to the spot where he'd left his clothes, pulled his hunting shirt on over his head, and raced back to where Daniel Boone stood giving orders to the men.

As he listened, John fumbled with his shirt, which reached nearly to his knees. He tied it up with the belt his mother had made and slipped his tomahawk beneath it on the right side and his knife beneath it on the left. He was ready for action.

Boone ordered several men to stay behind to protect the women and children. "It may be that they took the girls to draw us away from the fort."

"Don't worry, Dan'l. We'll guard the fort and keep the women and children safe," one of the young frontiersmen said.

Boone nodded his thanks.

Colonel Callaway, Fanny and Betsy's father, arrived on horseback. His nephew Flanders, John Holder, and a few others rode behind him. "We'll go downriver to a place where we can cross and meet you on the other side," Callaway called as they sped away.

The half-shaved Sam Henderson, John Floyd, and Floyd's friend Nathan Reid climbed into the dugout canoe.

"I'm sorry as can be, Dan'l," Nathan said. "I should have been with the girls."

"It's too late for regrets," Boone said. "Our job now is to bring the gals home."

The little dugout rocked back and forth.

John stood on the bank above the canoe. He tried to catch Captain Boone's eye to let him know he wanted to go along. After all, he was the one who fetched the canoe from the other shore. That should be worth something.

But there was no such invitation.

"We'll have to make a second trip," Boone said. He asked several men to wait by the riverbank, and he put John's dad, Captain Gass, in charge. "We'll send the dugout back for you."

Boone saluted and joined his men in the canoe.

Reid, who sat near the rear of the dugout, shouted, "Give us a push."

John rushed forward, lunged toward the dugout, and gave it a giant push.

And then he jumped in, landing on top of Nathan Reid.

"Whoa, boy!" Reid yelled, pushing John aside. "What do you think you're doing?"

Wasn't it obvious?

"I'm coming with you," John said. His voice broke, and he cringed. It seemed that whenever he wanted to sound strong, his voice betrayed him.

"Well then, move back a bit," Reid said.

Daniel Boone looked back, nodded, and smiled. "That's a fine idea. You can let us off and then go back to pick up the rest of the men."

"Yes, Sir," John said. He scrunched into the back of the dugout and took a deep breath. He'd been sure Reid would tell him to get lost, to stay on shore with the women and children. But he didn't, and Daniel Boone didn't either.

John remembered the proverb that his grandfather taught him: "The wicked flee when no man pursueth: but the righteous are bold as a lion."

I'm as bold as a lion.

It simply made sense to take control.

Act first. Explain later. That works for me.

The dugout moved swiftly through the water.

Captain Boone pointed to a spot about a quarter of a mile from the fort on the river's north shore. "They would have hidden in the canebrake there to take the girls."

The men rowed for the riverbank, and when they reached it, they jumped out. "Off you go," Boone said, and John turned the dugout around. He heard Daniel Boone tell the others to look for tracks. "Call out when you find them."

Golly, I wish I was already searching.

But John knew his task was important, too. He dipped the oars into the water and paddled smoothly. There was no splash at all as the dugout moved swiftly back toward the fort.

John cocked his ears, listening. It seemed unlikely that he'd hear the girls again, but he had to try. Birds TWEETED to one another. Frogs CROAKED near the shore, and when he rounded the bend, he could hear the MUMBLE of settlers gathered on the riverbank.

"Here's John!" his cousin yelled. "Did they find any sign of the girls?"

"Not yet."

48

Men on shore reached for the buffalo tug at the front of the dugout and pulled it in. They held it tight while several others climbed into the canoe. Big Tom grabbed the oars from John. "I'll handle this now," he said.

John sat tight.

I'm not staying behind. Act first! That's the key.

If needed, he would explain later. But it turned out that he didn't need to explain anything. Big Tom rowed swiftly away from shore. No one even suggested John stay behind.

John pointed and said, "Over there," when they reached the spot where Boone's group landed.

"Are you sure, son?" his father asked.

"Absolutely."

The men climbed out of the dugout. John tied the canoe to a stout young blue ash tree and followed the searchers ashore.

Captain Boone greeted them.

"We've yet to find any sign that the girls were here," he said. "We'll split into two groups and search until we find the trail. Callaway and his men will join us soon."

John squeezed in beside Captain Boone.

Boone sent John Floyd and Nathan Reid in one direction. John's dad and two others set off in another, and then Boone nodded to Sam Henderson, "You come with me."

And since no one said otherwise, John followed them.

It was Floyd and Reid who spotted the trampled cane where the girls had been captured.

John heard them shouting. "They've found the trail!" he yelled, and he took off running, determined to get there first.

But when he reached the river, he was alone. The voices had grown fainter, not louder. He found the dugout tied to the tree where they landed, but it wasn't where the girls had been taken. If it had been, they'd have spotted the trail sooner.

John stood still, his pulse racing, and listened.

PLOP! A fish jumped out of the water.

CAW! Four crows flew overhead.

CHIT! CHIT! CHITTER! Squirrels chatted in a nearby tree.

And then he heard a shout. "OVER HERE!"

He took a deep breath and sighed. The men!

John stumbled along the rocky bank and through a stand of cane. He slipped among the men as if he'd never left them. No one seemed to notice that he'd been missing or that he'd returned.

Golly, I shouldn't have worried. I knew I could find

'em.

A few minutes later, the mounted group arrived. Colonel Callaway rubbed his hands through his hair. "Why are we standing here doing nothing? The kidnappers are bound to harm the girls if they haven't already done so."

"No," Captain Boone said. "That's not the Shawnee way, and I have every reason to believe these men are Shawnee. They'll treat the girls as kindly as they would treat their own sisters. They'll want to adopt them into the tribe. Their numbers are dwindling. Disease has killed many, and they want to rebuild. They'll expect our girls to marry eligible young men and to become loyal members of the tribe."

"Not my girls," Captain Callaway said.

"Nor my Jemima," Boone added.

"Then we can't stand around doing nothing. My men and I will go after them on horseback. It's the fastest way to find them." Callaway turned away.

"Stop!" Boone said, putting his hands up. "You'll get them killed."

Callaway halted, his face twisted with anger. "Say what you mean."

Boone spoke slowly, his voice calm and quiet as he explained that the Indian custom was to keep one warrior well back of the main group. If anyone pursued them, the rear guard would warn the others. "Your horses will be noisy. They can't help it, and when the rear guard hears you, he'll alert the main party."

What then? John wondered. Would they hurt the girls?

"They'd rather kill the captives than give them up."

John cringed when he heard Captain Boone's words.

John lowered his head and rubbed his forehead.

If only I'd gone along. I coulda kept them safe.

Then he shook his head, aware that it probably wouldn't have mattered.

If only I had a gun . . . .

John stared at the ground. Then he heard Captain Boone say, "I have a plan."

John perked up and listened.

When Boone explained it, Richard Callaway agreed. Callaway's men would ride directly to the ford at the Licking River about 70 miles north. "The kidnappers will cross there on their way to the Shawnee villages," Boone explained. "Wait there. If we don't reach the girls first, you can ambush the kidnappers and recover the girls before they cross the river."

Meanwhile, Captain Boone explained that his group . . . .

My group. . .

. . . would track the girls through the forest—as quietly and cautiously as possible. With luck, they'd sneak up on the kidnappers and snatch the girls safely away.

John didn't hear a drop of doubt in Captain Boone's voice. He spoke confidently, certain the girls were still alive, and he intended to find them before they reached the Indian settlements.

Maybe there was still hope.

Callaway and the horsemen sped north.

John stayed close to Boone as they began tracking the captives. The sun was fading. Tangled underbrush made for slow going, especially since the men were still dressed in their Sunday best. Buckskin leggings, hunting shirts, and moccasins were better suited to the task, but no one, not a single man, had wanted to lose time changing out of his fancy togs.

RIP!

"My shirt," Sam Henderson said. It was torn near the shoulder. He pulled it away from the bush. "Seems we're not dressed for the hunt. You don't even have moccasins, Dan'l."

Boone looked down at his bare feet before looking back at Sam. "Tis so. I doubt the gals will care so long as we find 'em."

John followed the men into the wilderness.

THE FIRST DAY
Sunday, July 14, 1776
The Journey Begins

JEMIMA'S STORY

We go," The King said.

I'm sure I've seen him before.

He pointed north and led the way.

Jemima trudged along. Her feet may have dragged, but her mind was racing.

All I wanted was a bit of freedom. Freedom from the fort. Freedom from the family and their constant demands. And now, I may never be free again.

She stumbled.

"Move along," the one she called 'Mask' said from behind Jemima.

Moccasin walked in front of the group, just after The King.

Betsy was next, then Fanny, and finally, Jemima.

Bear followed behind them.

When Jemima turned to look at him, he frowned at her.

Maybe his head still hurts?

Red Paint stayed further back. Jemima's dad had told her that there's always a rear guard. It seemed Red Paint filled that role.

Jemima thought about what a strange procession they made. Cherokee and Shawnee warriors with three white girls dressed in their Sunday best, except for their legs, which were now wrapped in torn remnants.

If Mother could see us now. . . .

Jemima smiled at the thought. Her mother had raised her children in the wilderness and taught them to feel at home in the woods. Jemima never felt afraid when her mother was around. She knew that Rebecca Boone could handle any problem that might arise.

Oh, if only Mother was here! She'd know what to do.

The Boone cabin back in North Carolina sat on the edge of the forest. Jemima and her brothers and sisters played tag in the woods. They gathered firewood, herded the family cows, and helped with the farming. Her dad was often gone on long hunts, hunts that lasted months or even years, and it was up to her mother, Rebecca, and the children to keep the farm running. Like most girls her age, Jemima knew how to cook and sew and tend the younger children.

But she knew even more. She knew how to mark a trail. Daniel Boone was an expert tracker, but even so, he'd need whatever clues she could leave. She could picture him, calm and quiet, planning the rescue.

Bear nudged Jemima. "Go," he said, but Jemima stumbled and fell, anything to cause a delay. She had to give the searchers time to catch up. Speed was the enemy.

Step.

Pause.

Step.

Pause.

Step.

Stumble.

She'd do whatever it took to give her father time to catch up. There was no point in running, even if her foot allowed it. If only she could talk to Fanny and Betsy. She knew they would do whatever they could to help. But for now, she'd have to act first and explain later.

"Move along," Bear snarled. He gave Jemima the tiniest push, but it was enough to serve as an excuse.

She tumbled to the ground, screaming, and yelled as loudly as she could, "My foot! My poor, poor foot!" If her dad was tracking, and she was certain he was, he might be able to hear her.

When they heard Jemima's cries, Betsy and Fanny turned back and rushed to her side. They knelt and embraced Jemima, uttering words of sympathy.

"Delay," Jemima whispered to Betsy, "and mark the trail."

"We will," Betsy whispered back.

Fanny nodded in silent agreement.

They helped Jemima stand. She leaned on them, raising her sore foot so the men would notice.

"We go," Mask said, and the threat of knife and tomahawk urged the girls forward.

As she plodded on, Jemima's thoughts kept returning to her father. Daniel Boone was not a big man. He was of average height and weight, but he was far stronger than most men. His eyes were as blue as a summer sky, and his hair was sandy brown with red highlights. He wore it in a braid tied up to keep it secure beneath a hat made of beaver fur. He was a great hunter, perhaps the greatest hunter in the world, but Jemima knew that hunting bear or buffalo was not the same as hunting for three kidnapped girls.

Jemima and Fanny did what they could to distract the kidnappers. They pointed into the woods as if something lurked there. They called to one another—

"Are you well?"

"How are you doing?"

—which seemed to annoy the men. And whenever they crossed a buffalo wallow, Betsy dug deep gouges into the soft earth with her chunky wooden heels.

It took the men a while to notice what she was doing. When they did, Bear pulled her aside.

"No!" he said, his voice stern, and then he knocked the wooden heels off her shoes.

She tottered along on the uneven bottoms of her leather slippers. Jemima doubted that Betsy could leave gouge marks in the dirt without the heels, but she knew Betsy would try.

The kidnappers were experienced hunters. Jemima never doubted they were clever. They led the girls in and out of thick cane, through small streams, and across dry, rocky ground—tactics designed to hide their trail. Her dad, skilled tracker that he was, would have a hard time following them. She'd have to find some way to leave signs for the searchers.

It was Betsy who eventually came up with a solution. She tore bits of fabric from her dress, and ever so carefully, dropped them along the trail.

Jemima dipped her head to hide her smile. How clever!

Jemima was tempted to do the same, but what if one of the men noticed? She brushed against one of the prickly bushes lining the trail, hoping a bit of fabric would cling to the bush. When she snuck a glance back, there it was, just a tiny bit of cloth hanging off a pricker bush. It was a sign her father was bound to find.

Fanny reached out and broke a twig off a small tree. She dropped it on the trail.

Jemima did the same.

Moccasin noticed.

"We're tired," Fanny pleaded. "The branches help pull us along." It wasn't true, of course, but Jemima hoped this kind, soft-spoken man would believe it.

As the little band moved further inland, the kidnappers teased Bear about the blows the Callaway girls had dealt him with the paddle. He seemed to enjoy the teasing. The men laughed and joked with one another in Shawnee and listening to them was like listening to the young frontiersman at the fort. There was nothing frightening about the men themselves. They seemed kind enough, but that didn't mean that Jemima wanted to spend her life in a Shawnee village. Being forced to do something against her will wasn't her idea of freedom. Absolutely not.

Oh, please, Daddy. Hurry.

The men spoke to the girls in English.

She overheard Bear scold Fanny again. She didn't turn to look. Fanny had probably pulled on a branch near the path.

Good for you, Fanny.

Jemima reached out to twist a branch of her own.

It was a relief when the men finally stopped for a brief rest. The girls sat on the ground, with their backs to a giant oak. The men talked with one another. They seemed to be arguing, which gave the girls a chance to talk, although they were careful to keep their voices low. Jemima shared with them the names she'd given the men. "King, he's the older one, the one in charge. And Moccasin is much younger. He seems to be a gentle sort."

"He's the one who gave us the moccasins," Fanny said.

Jemima nodded. "And there's Bear, the one Betsy thought was *our* Simon, and Red Paint, and Mask."

Betsy hid her smile. "Now they have names, but we'd best keep them secret," she whispered. "They might not approve."

Jemima studied the men, especially the one who seemed familiar. He was older than the others, which is why she called him "King," and he was tall and sinewy. His dark eyes had an unexpected depth. Was he one of the men who'd come to the Boone cabin back in North Carolina? Indian hunters often stopped to talk to her father. They laughed and joked together. Sometimes they stayed for a meal. She remembered a time. . . .

Scolacutta? Yes, that was it.

In English, he was called Hanging Maw. He was an important Cherokee leader. Her Dad had said as much. And he was a friend.

A friend!

Once he knew who she was, he was bound to let her go. She imagined him saying, "It was all a mistake. I never meant to kidnap Boone's daughter." He might even take her back to Boonesborough and apologize for causing so much trouble.

"The King," Jemima pointed to Hanging Maw, "is a friend of my father's."

"A friend?" Fanny whispered.

Jemima nodded. "I have to tell him who I am."

"And what if he doesn't care?" Betsy asked. "My father says—"

Jemima shook her head, cutting Betsy off. "He will. I know he will."

Hanging Maw was kneeling, speaking with the other men, when Jemima stood and approached him. She took a deep breath and said, "I am Daniel Boone's daughter."

Hanging Maw straightened up. He studied Jemima's face, and then he reached out and stroked her long hair.

"Yes," he said, as if he recognized her. "And are these your sisters?"

Jemima nodded, hoping the lie would protect Betsy

and Fanny, too.

But Hanging Maw turned to the others and spoke to them in Cherokee. They all laughed, slapping their hands as if it was a great joke. "We have done pretty well for old Boone this time," he said in English, and the men laughed even louder. "We got all his young squaws."

THE FIRST DAY
Sunday, July 14, 1776
Twilight

JOHN'S STORY

John glanced at the sky. The sun was fading, and the path, shadowed by trees, grew dim. He felt itchy all over. Not mosquitos. Not poison ivy. Just worry. They didn't seem to be making any progress.

Golly. We'll soon lose the light, and if we can't see, how will we find the girls?

Tangled underbrush made the going slower too, as they trudged along the Warrior's Path, a centuries-old Indian hunting trail. John stayed as close to Captain Boone as possible. He didn't want to miss anything Boone might say. But Boone wasn't talking. No one was. The men moved silently through the woods, as silently as a herd of deer.

They traveled about five miles before the sun

dipped below the horizon leaving red streaks behind.

Suddenly, John yelled, "Listen!"

Boone reached out and clasped one hand over John's mouth. With the other, he put a finger to his lips.

John hung his head and gulped.

He'd said just one word.

Was it enough to give them away?

What if the Indians killed the girls all because of one word?

His word?

John reached for the nearest tree and grabbed onto it.

If only I could melt into the forest and disappear.

No wonder the frontiersmen treated him like a child. He suspected that even little Danny Boone would have known enough to keep quiet.

John thought of all the times he wanted to be noticed—and this time when he wished he hadn't been. He didn't dare look at Boone or his own dad.

He should just sneak away.

Go back to the fort.

But if he did that, they might think he'd been taken and start searching for him. What then? That would mean fewer men to track the girls.

No. I can't just leave.

All the men had stopped in their tracks. Boone bent

low, his eyes searching as best he could in the dark. He signaled the men forward. They crept along quietly, not even snapping any twigs. John lingered behind. For the first time in ages, he didn't want to be first.

An owl HOOTED.

A wolf HOWLED. John couldn't tell how close it was.

Not too close, I hope.

Boone stopped. "Listen," he whispered.

WOOF! WOOF!

The others heard it. This was no owl. It wasn't a wolf, either. The men followed the sound, and John followed the men.

A campfire glowed in the moonlight. A dog sat beside it. So did several men. A bright moon revealed the outline of a half-built cabin nearby.

John took a deep breath. It wasn't the kidnappers after all! These men were settlers.

Just like us.

He raced forward to join the others.

"We haven't seen anyone," one of the builders said in response to Captain Boone's question.

"Haven't heard anything either," another added.

And finally, John breathed easy. His shout hadn't done any harm. Not this time.

One of the men stepped forward.

"Why it's Billy Bush," Boone said to the others, and he turned to greet the man. "How do you fare?"

"Quite well, my friend. And what brings you here?"

Once Boone explained about the kidnapped girls, Billy said, "You must stay the night. There's no point in going on tonight. You won't be able to see the trail anyway. Wait and pick it up in the morning."

Boone nodded in agreement. "'Tis true. We'll stay."

The builders were happy for the company and more than willing to share the venison roasting on a spit over the campfire. There were no fancy dishes or silverware, but that didn't matter. The meat was tender and nourishing. John licked his fingers and eagerly accepted a second piece. There was no shortage of game in the Kentucky woods.

While he ate, he listened to what the men were saying.

"A couple of hunters came through here a week or so ago. They claimed that there was going to be a big conference at Chota."

"Chota?" John Floyd asked.

"The Cherokee capital," Boone explained. "It's their headquarters. All the military, political, and economic power of the Cherokee nation comes out of Chota. We've got no problem with the Cherokee," he added. "We negotiated with Attakullalulla at Sycamore Shoals last March and paid them well for this Kentucky land. Richard Henderson has the paper to prove it. It's the Shawnee that threaten us here in Kentucky."

"From what I hear," Billy Bush said, "Dragging Canoe, one of the young Cherokee chiefs invited the Shawnees to Chota. He plans to get them riled up. And not just the Shawnees. I heard tell they invited Delaware, Mohawk, Nanticokes, Ottawa, and maybe others to this gathering. I fear trouble's coming."

"Coming?" Sam Henderson said. "It's already here." He stood and paced back and forth.

"You think this kidnapping is part of the plan?" Nathan Reid asked.

"Maybe," Boone said. "That's why I left men to guard the fort. But maybe not. It could be that they saw the gals on the river and made a spur of the moment decision to grab 'em."

One of the others said, "Could be. But kidnapping women won't solve the problem unless it scares us back through the Cumberland Gap. Men like Dragging Canoe want us to leave Kentucky. And, if we're not careful, they'll side with the British when war breaks out."

John's dad nodded his head. "War's coming. That's certain."

War?

John had heard talk of high taxes and boycotts of

British goods, but he hadn't paid much attention. It was just talk, grown-up talk, although he did remember the day his father reported that some lads in Boston dumped a shipment of British tea into the ocean.

"Tea?" his mother had asked. "Now why would they do that?"

"To teach the British a lesson," Dad said. "They're boycotting British goods."

"That won't make any great difference to us," Mother said. "We get by with what we can make on our own. Fancy ladies in big Eastern cities may buy fabric from British merchants, but homespun serves as well if not better."

John fingered his hunting shirt. The fabric was rough but sturdy. His mother had been right. It served him well. When he looked at the men sitting around the fire, he noticed that Daniel Boone wasn't even wearing a shirt.

"I've seen enough of fighting," Boone said. He stretched his legs, wiggled his toes, and slapped a mosquito.

Golly! It isn't right for a man like Daniel Boone to search the woods half-naked.

He didn't even have moccasins. He needed a hunting shirt and leggings. They hadn't taken the time to pack food, either. It was pure luck that they had come upon the builders and been invited to join them. John had been feeling gut-foundered, and he knew the others had been hungry, too.

Even though the men were all great shots, they wouldn't have dared to shoot game. A gunshot was even louder than his yell.

I could go for supplies. I know the way. I'll be back before they even notice I'm gone.

He started to leave, to sneak away, but stopped and stared into the dancing flames. He was quiet, thinking.

Maybe that's not the best way.

John studied the men sitting around the fire. Brave men. Smart men.

What would they do?

THE FIRST DAY
Sunday, July 14, 1776
Twilight

JEMIMA'S STORY

The kidnappers didn't stop laughing. "We got old Boone this time."

Jemima hung her head and limped back to Betsy and Fanny. She heard the word *Boone* several more times, and her disappointment turned to anger.

How dare they laugh at my daddy?

He'd been a friend to Hanging Maw. Her mother had fed him at the family table. And the others? Her dad would have welcomed them into his cabin, too.

If only I hadn't said anything . . . .

Betsy and Fanny wrapped their arms around Jemima. "Do not be troubled," Betsy said. "You tried to help."

It was little comfort. She was afraid she'd made

things even worse—if that was possible.

*Dear God in Heaven Above, help my father find us.
And hurry.*

She sighed and tried to swallow, but her throat
was dry. So dry. She hadn't had anything to drink since
they started walking. She studied her hands. They were
bruised from falling along the trail. She brushed away
what dirt she could, but her hands didn't come clean.

"A little dirt won't do any harm," Betsy said.

Fanny leaned close and whispered. "They'll come
for us. I know they will."

Jemima looked into her friend's eyes and saw a
spark of hope.

"Yes, Jemima said, letting the anger seep away.
"They will."

When Hanging Maw said, "We go," Fanny and
Betsy pulled Jemima to her feet.

It had been a long day, and all three were exhausted. Now it was getting late.

The trees along the trail cast eerie shadows as
Jemima trudged along, footsore and weary.

She fingered the fabric in her dress. She'd been
so proud of that dress, and now it was ruined. Tears
threatened when she thought about her mother and the
worry she was causing. She was surprised at how much
she longed to return to Boonesborough, the very place

she had wanted to escape only a few hours earlier.

Jemima had to admit that from time to time she complained about all the chores frontier life demanded. She helped Mother with cooking, cleaning, washing, sewing, fetching water, planting gardens, chasing younger brothers and sisters, herding cows, and tending the hogs.

I'll never complain again, if only I can return home.

She tried not to think of what might lay ahead. Instead, she focused on what lay behind: Boonesborough. It was neither a city nor a town, but it was home. It was not even a village. There were no elegant houses with comfortable furniture. The Boone's cabin was one of a half dozen rough-built log homes. Forests surrounded the settlement on three sides. The Kentucky River ran past the fourth. The settlers called Boonesborough a fort, but it was only half-built. The windowless backs of many of the cabins formed the outside walls. Eventually, the settlers planned to build high stockades between the cabins to make the fort secure. There was always work to do.

One of the cabins was used to store flour, ammunition, and other basic supplies. It was the closest Boonesborough had to a store. There were no shops where Jemima could buy new shoes or ready-made dresses. The nearest shops that sold fancy goods were at least 500 miles away in Williamsburg, Virginia.

Her Dad had been there, and he reported that the governor lived in a mansion. He said there was a courthouse, a parish church, and dozens of shops. Jemima could only imagine the variety of cloth in lovely colors and varied designs. There were apothecary shops, too, that sold medicines, and places to buy candles and soap, things she and her mother had to make themselves or wait until someone returned with supplies.

Boonesborough didn't have a doctor, either, to treat Jemima's sore foot. In emergencies, the settlers depended on one another.

This was an emergency. A major emergency!

There was no cavalry to come to the rescue, but Jemima was certain that her dad and Colonel Callaway would be searching. She couldn't allow herself to get discouraged, not again.

They will come. Yes, they will.

If she thought it enough, it would be true.

They will come.

She thought of Flanders. He was about the same height as her dad, 5 feet 10 inches tall, and lean like the kidnappers. His hair was as dark as Jemima's, and his eyes were deep-set and midnight black. He was thoughtful, quiet. He never said much, but he didn't need to. Jemima knew he liked her as much as she liked him.

Flanders would be searching, too, but would he arrive in time?

Even though the night air was warm, Jemima shivered. Fanny was walking even more slowly than Jemima. Although Fanny was a few months older, she was not as tall nor as strong as Jemima. Even Betsy was sagging.

As the sun disappeared behind the trees, Hanging Maw called a halt. "We rest here," he said.

Jemima's stomach grumbled. Now that they stopped, she was sure they'd light a campfire and cook some meat. Her spirits rose, at least a bit, and it wasn't only the thought of food. A fire would serve as a beacon. Her dad would follow the smoke, even if he didn't see the fire and smell the roasting meat.

But the kidnappers didn't light a fire. There was no fresh meat. They pulled pieces of dried buffalo tongue out of their pockets and offered some to the girls. "Eat!" Mask said. He sat down and gnawed on the jerky. The other men concentrated on the food, only occasionally looking over at the girls.

Jemima prodded the buffalo tongue with a dirty finger. It was solid, as hard as the ground she sat on. She slowly lifted it to her mouth. Over the years, she'd eaten lots of smoked meat. The meat her father smoked was tasty, but when she touched this jerky to her tongue and tried to chew, it was like chewing a stick and just as

74

tasteless.

Fanny had apparently managed to bite off a chunk. She spat it out.

Betsy tossed hers on the ground.

The kidnappers laughed. They spoke rapidly in Shawnee and laughed some more. Jemima gave them the evil eye, which only made them laugh harder.

She stood up.

Bear lifted his tomahawk in one hand and motioned her back to the ground with the other.

Why does he seem so angry? It's not like we're going to escape.

She sat again, but this time, she settled closer to Betsy and Fanny.

Betsy pulled the girls together and whispered, "Sam will be on our trail. I know he will."

"Father, too," Fanny said.

Jemima only nodded. They all knew that Daniel Boone would be tracking them. "Tomorrow. They'll find us tomorrow," she said and prayed she was right.

THE FIRST NIGHT
Sunday, July 14, 1776

JOHN'S STORY

By the time John had devised a plan, the men were leaving the campfire to bed down for the night. John turned to Captain Boone. All that thinking led to one conclusion.

Ask first and then act.

He screwed up his courage. "Sir," he said. "I'd like your permission to return to the fort for supplies." He looked at Captain Boone's bare feet and pantaloons.

Boone cocked his head toward John. Was he remembering what happened earlier? John knew he'd never make that mistake again. No more shouting. No matter what.

"I can do it, Sir," John said. "Please let me try."

Boone looked to John's dad. "David?" he asked.

Captain Gass nodded. "Send the boy," he said.

"Then go, Lad, and if you succeed, we'll all be in your debt. It's ammunition we need, as well as any victuals they can spare. We've brought little food with us. And remember, we leave at first light. If you're not here . . . ."

"I'll be here," John said. "Thank you, Sir."

"Godspeed," Captain Boone said.

John took a few minutes to gather several cane stalks. He bound them together to form a torch and dipped it into the fire. It would help light his way to the river, not that he'd need it. Still, it would please his Dad to see him use the torch as he'd been taught to do.

It was at least five miles to the river where the dugout was tied. Once he reached it, he'd take the dugout to the fort and return. The trip might take all night.

"Sam," Boone said, and without another word, Sam Henderson fell in beside John.

"I can't sleep. I can't sit still. All I can think about is Betsy and what may befall her. I might as well go for a stroll," Sam said.

Their pace was much quicker than a stroll. John was eager to get the supplies and return in plenty of time to resume the search. If he ran, he might even get a few hours' sleep.

He was relieved when Sam turned back after a

couple of miles. All Sam could talk about was Betsy. Betsy this. Betsy that. John's mom would say that Sam was moonstruck. His head was full of romantic ideas, and that made him too worried about Betsy to be good company.

The moon shone brightly through the trees, and the sky sparkled with stars. John wasn't alone. The forest was a noisy place.

Crickets CHIRPED. It was a comfortable sound. Usually, it lulled him to sleep.

Then something GROWLED.

A bear?

John hurried along until he heard a raccoon CHITTER and HISS.

Good!

A raccoon would never linger near a bear unless it wanted to become lunch. John took a deep breath and slowed down.

When he held his torch high, John saw two bright yellow eyes staring back at him. He could see the rack.

Deer! A buck.

John didn't move, and the buck came closer. It lowered its head to eat.

John crept toward the deer.

It raised its head.

John stood absolutely still. It was a game he'd

played before. A good hunter crept close to a deer so his shot would be true.

But I'm not hunting. Not now.

He gave up the game and sauntered along the trail to the river. He had a different goal on this particular night.

His torch was burning low, but he no longer needed it. When he heard a beaver BARKING and GNAWING, he knew he was near water. He reached the patch of cane where the search had begun. The dugout was still there, tied to the tree.

John untied it and hopped in. He paddled the short distance back to Boonesborough.

The fort was easy to spot in the bright moonlight. John tied the dugout to a tree beside the river and climbed the steep bank. He started across the meadow between the river and the fort and then darted into the cornfield.

What if there's a guard? What if the guard thinks I'm an enemy planning to attack?

John peered through the tall corn stalks. A guard slumped on the ground against one of the fort's palisades. For just an instant, John thought the man was dead.

Wounded? Had there been an attack?

And then the guard roused himself and stretched,

his long arms outspread.

"Halloo!" John called. This time he felt free to shout. Sneaking up on the guard might mean death.

"Who goes there?"

"John Gass. I've come for supplies."

"Come!" the man called, and John hurried forward.

"It's Little John Gass!" the guard called into the fort, and several women, including his own mother, came running to meet him.

Mrs. Boone rushed out of the Callaway's cabin. "Have you news?" she asked.

Mrs. Callaway appeared behind her. "Oh, please," Mrs. Callaway begged. "Tell us they've found the girls."

John hung his head. "No, Ma'am. They'll resume the search tomorrow. I've come to fetch supplies. Proper togs and ammunition. Food, if you can spare it."

The women hurried away to gather what they could. Mrs. Boone gave John a satchel with her husband's moccasins, a hunting shirt, his breechcloth, and leggings. Mrs. Callaway brought jerked venison, and several of the frontiersmen emptied their powder and shot into a hunting pouch. His mother gave him a bag of berries that the children had collected.

One of the frontiersmen offered to return with him.

"You're needed here," John said. "I'll be fine alone."

They all wished him luck and sent him back into

the night.

He paddled quickly. The moon reflected off the river water. It seemed nearly as bright as day. He rowed ashore, tied the dugout securely, and started back toward the campsite where the men lay sleeping.

The supplies weighed him down, but John had a purpose. He ran as swiftly as a young deer. As quietly, too. Nothing would stop him. Not even a bear.

He heard the CRASH of tree branches as some animal pushed through the forest.

A buffalo. But not a big one. Maybe a calf looking for its mother.

He didn't stop to check. He kept going. He had no light. He couldn't see the path, but he felt the smoothness of it through his moccasins. Herds of animals, deer, elk, and buffalo had polished it free of roots and undergrowth. That night, John's feet were more useful than his eyes.

He stopped beside a large tree and rubbed his hand over the bark. On the opposite side, he felt moss. Its softness reassured him that he was headed in the right direction: north. Every frontier boy knew that moss grew on the north side of trees.

It was well before dawn when he reached the camp. He laid the supplies near the fire, where a few coals still glimmered, and then he lay down for a few hours rest.

THE FIRST NIGHT
Sunday, July 14, 1776

JEMIMA'S STORY

After sundown, Hanging Maw called a halt for the night.

At least we can rest for a spell. Sleep will bring a kind of freedom.

But that wasn't to be.

By the time the men finished eating the dried buffalo tongue, it was totally dark. The kidnappers tied each girl to a separate tree. They pinioned the girls' arms behind their backs, so they couldn't reach the ropes to untie them. The ropes prevented them from lying down, too, so they were forced to sit upright. Their backs rubbed against jagged tree bark.

While the kidnappers slept peacefully at their feet, the girls stared into the dark and worried. As tired as she was, Jemima couldn't sleep. Neither could Betsy nor Fanny. If they nodded to sleep, their necks fell forward and jerked them awake. They didn't dare whisper for fear of waking the sleeping men.

Jemima listened to night sounds. An owl hooted. Another one barked, a low "woof, woof," almost like a dog. Crickets chirped. The peeps of frogs told her that there was water nearby, maybe a pond or a small creek. Something screamed, and Jemima leaned back against the tree by instinct, not that the tree offered any protection. It was unlikely that a bobcat or coyote would attack, not once it picked up the smell of humans. Even so, the scream was unsettling.

Jemima's foot hurt. She thought of her mother, who had rubbed a paste of comfrey root and slippery elm bark onto the cut. Ma knew which roots and plants to use as medicine. She knew as much about farming as Daniel did, probably more because he was often away. It was her mother who took care of the gardens, planting sweet potatoes, squash, and pumpkins. Jemima helped with the planting, the weeding, and the harvesting. All the Boone children did.

Jemima's thoughts turned to her brothers and sisters. To James, dead now for two years, to Israel, who spent his time hunting and exploring with the other frontiersmen at the fort, and to Susannah, who was two years older than Jemima. Susannah was already married to William Hays, and off on an adventure of her own. She'd been with William and her dad when they'd cut the path through the Cumberland Gap to Boonesbor-ough. Jemima wondered exactly where Susannah and William were and what they were doing.

Likely wandering free.

She wished it was true for her, too.

With Susannah gone, the younger girls counted on Jemima. Lavinia was nine, and Rebecca had just turned seven. They looked up to her, and so did the little boys, Danny and Jesse. They made her laugh with their silly antics, and she loved snuggling in next to her sisters each night in the loft as they lay on the buffalo robe they used as a mattress.The chores no longer mattered.

Even being forted was better than being a prisoner.

Jemima didn't need to be told where she and the Callaways were headed. They were going north to the Shawnee villages on the Ohio River. They'd be adopted into the tribe. She'd be separated forever from the family she loved.

Please, Daddy. Hurry!

She repeated the words silently over and over like a kind of chant.

He must be searching. She'd seen her dad deal with one crisis after another. He was a clever man, a calm and careful man, a man who always came up with a plan.

He'd been a captive, too, and lived to talk about it. Jemima was only six-and-a-half years old when her dad returned to their North Carolina home to tell the story, but she never forgot what he said. He hadn't told the story just once either. He told it over and over.

"It was in May 1769, that I left my peaceful home and my family in North Carolina to wander through the wilderness of America, in quest of the country of Kentucky. We found an abundance of wild beasts of all sorts through the vast forests. The buffaloes were more numerous than the cattle back in the settlements. They grazed on the leaves of cane that grew everywhere or nibbled grasses in the meadow lands. They were fearless, because they were unaware of the violence of man. Sometimes we saw hundreds, and the numbers around the salt springs were amazing. The forests were the home to beasts of every kind natural to America, and so we hunted with great success until December the 22nd.

"On that day, John Stewart and I had a pleasing ramble through a great forest. There were countless trees, some with blossoms, others rich with fruit. Nature was here a series of wonders and a fund of delight. We were overcome with the beauty of nature—the beautifully colored flowers and the delicious fruits—and by the number and variety of animals. At the close of the day, near the Kentucky River, we reached the top of a small hill when a number of Indians rushed out of a thick cane-brake and made us their prisoners. They took the furs that we had gathered and held us prisoners for seven days.

We never tried to escape, which made them less suspicious of us. We relaxed and tried to act as if we were quite content to remain with them.

However, on the 7th night, we camped in a thick cane-brake by a large fire. I was troubled by our captivity, missing my family, and fearful that I might never return, so sleep did not come. I listened to the heavy breathing of the others, and when I realized the men all around me were sleeping soundly, I touched Stewart gently to wake him. We took the opportunity to escape. When we returned to the camps where our hunting companions had been, we found that their camps had been plundered and they had all gone home."

Jemima sat up straight. She wanted to share her thoughts with the Callaways, but Betsy had nodded off, and Fanny was too far away.

It was simple, really: If Daniel Boone could escape, they could, too.

She took a deep breath and leaned back against the tree. It was then that she remembered something else her father told her about a second capture and a second escape. When he found the camp plundered, he didn't give up. He returned to the Shawnee camp to steal the pelts back. He told her that he and Stewart waited until after dark, and as the Indians slept, they crept back into camp. They stole four or five of their own horses and raced away.

The Shawnee chief was outraged. He set off with a dozen mounted warriors, tracked Boone down, and captured him for the second time. This time, the Shawnees set out to teach Boone a lesson.

They hung one of the horse's bells around his neck and made him dance. The bells jingled merrily as Daniel danced a jig, which made the Shawnees laugh and hoot. It struck them as very funny.

A few days later, when the warriors were busy setting up camp, he and Stewart dashed into the thick cane again. They were free.

Her daddy had waited until exactly the right moment, and he escaped. Twice.

I only have to do it once—and take Fanny and Betsy with me.

They'd have to be patient like her dad had been. There was no point in trying to get away too soon. Meanwhile, they'd keep up the delaying tactics, and when the time was right, she and the Callaway girls would break free!

THE SECOND DAY
Monday, July 15, 1776
Dawn

JOHN'S STORY

John had been sleeping for less than two hours when he felt a hand on his shoulder.

"Wake up, lad." Captain Boone said.

John opened his eyes and stood up. "Did you find the supplies?" he asked.

"We did." Captain Boone spread his arms to show off his hunting togs, and then he pointed to his moccasins. "You did well. We'll be off soon enough. Rest a bit and then you can return to the fort."

"Oh, no, Sir," John said loud enough that others turned to stare. He jumped up, brushing moss from his shirt. "Please don't send me back. I want to help with the search."

"But you were up all night. You've done more than

your part."

"Please, Sir. Let me go with you. I won't hold you back. I promise. I can do it."

Daniel Boone rubbed his chin and smiled. "I savvy that. You remind me of myself when I was a lad. Come along."

John smiled. Daniel Boone not only understood how he was feeling, but he also trusted him to keep up. And he would. There was no way he would let Captain Boone or his own dad down.

John laced up his moccasins, tied his belt around his waist, and belted his knife and tomahawk.

Today we find the girls.

He was sure of it.

Three of the cabin builders joined the search party.

At first, the trail was easy to follow. Within a few hours, the searchers found the spot where the kidnappers had camped for the night. But soon after, the trail disappeared.

The men strained to see tracks that did not exist. Daniel Boone cocked his head to listen. So did John.

Squirrels CHITTERED and SKITTERED from branch to branch.

Birds flew off, SQUAWKING in outrage.

Several of the men spoke up. "We've lost the trail." But Captain Boone reassured them. "I know their ways," he said. "Trust me."

John did, and it appeared that the frontiersmen did as well. After all, Daniel Boone's years of experience had taught him the habits and customs of native hunters.

Around noon they came to a small pond. Daniel Boone ordered a brief rest, and while they were sitting near the water, he spoke of his own childhood:

"I was about John's age when I began hunting alone in the woods of Pennsylvania. I learned about the woods and the animals living there from Indian hunters: Tuscaroras, Tutelas, Conoys, and Nanticokes. Shawnees, too, and Susquehannocks. They were my teachers, kind men, who showed me how to prepare hides and furs.

"They taught me a thing or two about healing, too. They knew all the medicinal plants: what made a cut heal faster, what soothed a burn, what eased the pain of the dying.

"We lived in peace then, as I pray we will in the future. But I recall the saying of the old chief who signed Colonel Henderson's deed, the one giving us this land to settle.

Taking me by the hand, 'Brother,' says he, 'we have

given you a fine land, but I believe you will have much
trouble settling it."

Boone stood, ready to resume the hunt. "They'll
disguise their route. You'll see. They'll walk through
water and thick underbrush.

"Is there no hope?" Sam Henderson asked, his
voice quaking with emotion. John expected him to start
moaning about Betsy, but for once Sam held his tongue.

"We wouldn't be here if it was hopeless. We'll find
'em, but I don't see much point in searching for a hidden
trail. We'll head across country directly toward the ford
at the Licking River. That's where they'll cross on their
way to the Shawnee villages. And that's where Callaway
and his men will be waiting. Remember the further they
get from Boonesborough, the more confident they'll
become. Sooner or later, we'll find more signs."

Some of the men protested."It's safer staying on the
Warrior's Path," Sam Henderson said.

"Safer, maybe," John's dad said, "but I say we follow
Dan'l."

John agreed. He almost spoke up, but he stopped
and thought before he said anything.

He decided it was best to stay quiet and listen.

Those who disagreed gave in. They knew Daniel
Boone had spent years in the woods, and no one wanted
to find the girls more than he did, except maybe Sam

Henderson, who kept whining about "poor Betsy."

After going cross-country for several miles, Captain Boone stopped suddenly. He lifted a hand, put his finger to his lips, and signaled the men to gather round. "Shoe print. Leather sole. With the heel missing."

"It's Betsy's," Sam whispered. "I'd know those fancy shoes anywhere. She was wearing them Sunday morning at the river."

"Good Man," Boone said. "That's information we can use."

It was John who found a bit of fabric clinging to the bushes.

"Look!" he cried, until his father told him to shush saying, "Don't give us away, Lad."

John turned away, ashamed of his outburst.

What's wrong with me? Will I never learn?

Captain Boone reached for the cloth. "Another sign," he said, patting John on the shoulder. "And no harm done this time. I suspect they're well ahead of us."

"Look for signs, Boys," he told the searchers. And, sure enough, bits of fabric clung to bushes and branches along the way. It was just as Daniel Boone predicted: they were going in the right direction.

But were they too late?

THE SECOND DAY
Monday, July 15, 1776
Dawn

JEMIMA'S STORY

Sunlight filtered through the trees. Jemima blinked, desperate to rub her eyes, but her arms were still tied.

The kidnappers stirred. They stood and stretched.

Jemima watched with envy. She tried to shrug her shoulders, but the tight ropes prevented even that.

Finally, Moccasin untied her.

"It's about time," Jemima said, no longer caring if she sounded grouchy, but Moccasin only laughed.

She brushed him away and rubbed her arms. When she extended them, she noticed the blood on her sleeves, some patches still wet. Her struggles against the ropes during the night had caused jagged cuts and scratches that bled onto the white sleeves of her dress. She noticed a long white string dangling from her skirt where the men had cut it to make leggings.

When she was little, she used to tie knots in strings like this. It was a game she played with her older sister, Susannah. That was ages ago.

Will I ever be so carefree again?

She glanced at Fanny and Betsy. They looked as miserable as she felt. Betsy yawned. Fanny stomped her feet up and down. They had fallen asleep even if the rest of her hadn't.

"We go," Hanging Maw said.

"No," Jemima said quietly as she hobbled toward the Callaway girls. When she reached them, she whispered, "Delay." She knew they knew, but she had to say it, if only to reassure herself.

"Be strong," Betsy said, reaching out to stroke Jemima's long hair. Her bonnet had long since fallen off, although Jemima had no idea when and where. Luckily, she hadn't lost the combs, which kept the hair out of her face.

Fanny took Jemima's hand in her own. "They'll come," she said, and Jemima nodded. "And if not. . . ."

We'll escape.

"Enough talk," Hanging Maw said, and this time, Jemima hobbled along behind Bear, who led the way. She watched how lightly he walked, barely disturbing the ground. He was a man of the forest, fit and strong. She could picture him running as gracefully as a young buck, leaping over fallen trees and vanishing into the forest. He was taller by a head than she was and so much stronger. He seemed less angry now. He even smiled from time to time. Even so, escape seemed impossible. How could three girls possibly outrun these strong, powerful men?

The kidnappers pushed the girls hard. They didn't stop for food or drink, and when they caught the girls trying to mark the trail, they threatened them with their knives.

The threat reminded Jemima of the small knife she had put into her pocket Sunday morning. It was just a kitchen knife, one she used to cut corn and meat, but it might be sharp enough to slice through the ropes binding them.

She glanced around. The Indians were talking and joking with one another, not paying any attention to the girls.

It was little wonder she'd forgotten about the knife. It was about the length of her index finger. The pocket holding it was a separate piece of cloth carried inside her dress. Carefully, she reached into the dress and pulled the knife from the hidden pocket. Her hand caught on the string that dangled from her skirt.

The game!

It wasn't just a game anymore. It might be the clue her Dad needed.

It's worth a try.

She rubbed her finger across the blade. It wasn't sharp enough to do much harm, but it would certainly cut the string.

Snip!

She hurriedly shoved the knife back inside her pocket.

As they walked along, she tied five knots in the string.

Five knots.

Five kidnappers.

If her dad spotted the string, he'd know what it meant.

She waited until no one was looking and limped to the side of the trail. She grabbed a branch.

Fanny, who realized what Jemima was doing, studied to distract the men. She pointed to her own muddy legs and skirts and called to Betsy, "Look at me. What would mother say?"

The kidnappers turned toward Fanny.

Good for Fanny.

While everyone was distracted, Jemima hung the string from a branch. It was nearly invisible.

If anyone can spot it, Daddy can.

She prayed that the kidnappers wouldn't notice it. When Jemima looked back, the men were still watching the Callaways. Betsy was looking stern and wagging her finger at Fanny.

"Yes, that is exactly what Mother would do," Fanny said.

Jemima returned to the trail. None of the men seemed to have noticed that she'd stepped aside.

Done! If only Daddy sees it. . . .

She'd have to wait until later to thank the girls for their help.

Jemima rubbed muddy hands on her torn apron. She quickly joined the conversation. "We make a pretty picture. Tis a good thing we have no looking glass."

Fanny giggled. "If we had, we'd be sure to break it."

The men glanced at the giggling girls, and they began to laugh, too.

Jemima winked at Fanny.

We did it!

"Enough fun," Hanging Maw said. "We have a long trip ahead."

Jemima was no stranger to travel on rough trails. It was only ten months earlier that her family left North Carolina to cross the Cumberland Mountains into Kentucky. Her dad and a group of rugged frontiersmen had marked the trail a few months before. It was more a path than a road. They called it Boone's Trace.

It wasn't even wide enough for wagons. Packhorses carried supplies. Little children rode horseback and babies rode in baskets dangling from the horses' sides. Sometimes the settlers piled supplies onto the cows. It worked better than trying to carry a pile of pots and pans in their arms.

Jemima had walked ahead of the horses with the other children. They herded the cows and pigs along the trail. The Callaways didn't arrive at the fort until weeks later, so it was John Gass who kept Jemima company on the long journey. Her younger sisters trailed after them. Her brother Danny ran off with the other little boys, but they never strayed far from the trail. The frontiersmen serving as guards made sure of that.

Jemima had waded across rivers and streams, climbed up the Cumberland Mountains, passed through the Cumberland Gap, and slid down the other side. She circled swamps, jumped over creeks, and squished through mud. All in all, she traveled over 300 miles in just a few weeks.

Even so, the journey to Boonesborough had been a happy, trouble-free journey promising new beginnings and new adventures.

This journey, in contrast, felt like the end of

everything she had ever known. Her foot hurt. The ropes had rubbed her skin raw, and even her stomach growled in protest.

Soon after she left the knotted string on the branch, they stopped at a spring to drink. Jemima knelt in the mud and scooped the water with her hands. It was so hot and humid that she wanted to sink into the mud and take a cool nap.

Betsy urged her to rise, with a nod to Bear, whose tomahawk pointed back toward the trail. "We don't have a choice."

Jemima nodded. She rubbed her thumb over the tiny knife in her hidden pocket. It gave her courage. She knew she had to be brave and stay alert. It was the only way.

Be strong.

Either Daddy will find us or we'll escape.

THE SECOND DAY
Monday, July 15, 1776
Mid-Afternoon

JOHN'S STORY

They'd been traipsing through the woods for hours. John wiped the sweat from his forehead. "Golly, it's hot!" he said.

The others were hot, too, but no one suggested stopping to rest. John didn't either. He was as focused on finding the girls as anyone, except perhaps Daniel Boone or Sam Henderson.

"Look at this!" Nathan Reid said. "It must be Miss Betsy's."

Sam rushed forward and took the cloth in hand. It was a small piece of Betsy's hanky, with an *E* for *Elizabeth*, her full name, embroidered in the corner. The men gathered round. Finding the bit of cloth cheered them.

"We're on their trail for sure," one said.

"Good catch," Boone said, his voice almost too soft to hear. "Keep your eyes open, Men. Anything unusual may be a sign."

Boone put a hand on Sam's shoulder. "I know you want to stick to this trail, but that would be an error." He insisted that they take the most direct line to the Ohio where the Shawnee villages were located. "That's where they'll be going," Boone said, and there was no doubt in his voice, none at all. He'd been right earlier, and it was likely that he was still right.

No one disagreed. "We go fast and quiet," Boone said. "Keep close together now. And remember, in the country, never look for Indians. Instead, keep a sharp lookout for their guns lying across logs or fallen timber."

John paid close attention. It was an important lesson. He'd be watching, but not just for guns. If he saw anything, anything at all out of the ordinary, he'd let Captain Boone know.

Boone led the way. He didn't waste time. Even the young frontiersmen struggled to keep up. They didn't say a word, but they panted like big, furry buffaloes as they charged through the forest.

At times they followed the Warrior's Path. John overheard Captain Boone telling Nathan Reid about following this path during his long hunts.

Later, they veered away from the trail, traipsing

through tall stands of cane before taking a buffalo trace that paralleled the Warrior's path. Buffalo had made the path over the years, but there were fewer and fewer buffalo in the forests of Kentucky by the time the settlers arrived. Earlier, though, Captain Boone said, he's seen thousands grazing in western Kentucky bluegrass country.

Oh, to be an explorer.

Someday, John vowed, he'd travel West to where the buffalo roamed. He stood still for a full minute, imagining the sight, only to look up and see the rest of the men disappear into the distance.

John ran, thrashing through the heavy brush. His legs were burning. His feet grew heavier with each step. He couldn't give up. He simply couldn't. He'd begged to come along. How could he stop now? He closed his eyes for just a moment but snapped them open when he felt himself falling asleep—even though he was still standing up. The muscles in his legs twitched.

The men sprinted further and further ahead.

THE SECOND DAY
Monday, July 15, 1776
Mid-Afternoon

JEMIMA'S STORY

Jemima's mind felt fuzzy as she lifted one foot and then the other. They'd been walking for hours. "Too tired," she said. She didn't bother to add that she was hungry, too—absolutely gut-foundered. But the last thing she wanted was the offer of tough and tasteless buffalo tongue. She supposed it was kindly meant. They shared what they had, but when her mom cooked meat, it was as tender as mashed squash and went down just as easily.

"Faster," Hanging Maw said. "We must go faster."

Jemima tripped and fell. On purpose. Moccasin helped her up. He shook his head in sympathy, but he never said a word. She'd been falling since they were first taken.

Did he think I'm clumsy? Probably, but so be it.

The goal was to delay the trip, and it seemed to be working.

Jemima brushed herself off and resumed walking. She dragged her sore and weary feet. At least, she thought, we're leaving footprints. But when she looked back, she saw Red Paint using a leafy branch to wipe away any footprints left behind.

Suddenly Bear stopped and pointed toward an open meadow where a small white pony was grazing. "Look!"

The others did as Bear said. They became excited. "Yes! Girls ride," Hanging Maw said.

The horse would speed the journey. Jemima would no longer limp along and complain. She would stop that annoying falling and screaming.

Even Jemima rejoiced at first. She loved riding horseback. She'd been doing it since she was a toddler. But it only took a minute for her to realize that she couldn't accept this particular kindness. Her plan was to delay, and that hadn't changed.

Hanging Maw motioned for Jemima to hop on the pony.

She didn't move.

"Ride horseback," he said again, and when Jemima stubbornly refused, Moccasin and Mask lifted her onto the pony's back.

She slid off screaming in fake pain.

Thud!

Betsy and Fanny ran to her side, comforting her. Betsy winked, a sign that she and Fanny knew exactly what had happened.

But the kidnappers didn't. They gently helped Jemima back onto the horse. They even sat Fanny behind her as support, and they seemed to assume that the problem was solved.

This time, both girls tumbled off the pony, yelling as they fell.

The kidnappers laughed. They shook their heads and slapped one another on the back. They were laughing at her, but also at her father, who apparently hadn't bothered to teach his daughters how to ride a horse.

"They think we can't ride," Fanny whispered to Jemima.

Jemima smiled. "Good. Let 'em."

"Try again," Hanging Maw said. They seemed determined to make use of the unexpected gift of a horse.

This time strong arms lifted all three girls onto the pony's back.

Fanny pinched the pony's rump.

It bared its teeth.

Betsy jabbed her heels into the pony's side. When she slid off, the pony bit her on the arm.

Betsy shrieked. The wound was not deep, but it was painful.

Fanny fell off next, and then Jemima tumbled to the ground.

Jemima expected to see tomahawks raised, but that didn't happen. The men shook their heads, but they remained patient. They were as determined as ever to take advantage of the horse. Finally, Mask said, "I will show you. It's a good horse."

He climbed onto the pony's back. He gave it a strong whack with the handle of his tomahawk. It didn't buck. It didn't bite. The pony stood still, as if waiting for further orders.

"See. It is a fine horse."

Hanging Maw turned to the girls. "You try again."

Red Paint helped lift the three girls onto the pony's back.

The horse began moving forward.

The kidnappers looked pleased. They smiled and nodded . . . .

. . . and then all three girls tumbled to the ground, yelling as they fell. They stood up slowly, a bit bruised, but rather pleased with the trouble they were causing.

"Enough!" Hanging Maw swatted the pony's haunches and sent it back to the meadow.

The kidnappers and their captives trudged slowly

forward on foot.

Jemima winked at Fanny. They had definitely slowed things down, and they had the bruises to prove it.

"We're lucky," Betsy whispered. "Others have been killed for less."

Jemima shivered. Betsy spoke truth. It was hard to agree that being kidnapped was lucky, but the men had been kind, at least as kind as they could be under the circumstances.

THE SECOND DAY
Monday, July 15, 1776
Evening

JOHN'S STORY

John fought desperately to keep up with the others. He was panting. His legs cramped, but he didn't dare stop to rest.

I can do it. I have to.

Daniel Boone raced through the dense forest. He was the oldest by far, but age didn't slow him down. John was relieved to see one of the other men lag behind. So long as he kept that man in sight, he'd eventually reach the others.

John's legs churned through the cane as he tried to catch up. Running through the woods reminded him of chasing pigs. Back in North Carolina, the family pigs had foraged in the woods. They ate acorns, beechnuts, and roots of all kinds. Whenever his mother wanted ham or bacon, she sent John after a pig. Wolves and bears killed a few, but most survived. Their skin was so tough that not even rattlesnakes could kill them. In fact, John had once seen a pig eat a snake alive. It squirmed and wriggled all the way into the pig's mouth.

When John told his cousins, the boys laughed. "So, I suppose when we eat pig, we're also eating snake!" one of them said.

"I hear that snake tastes like chicken," another added, which set them to laughing all over again.

Thinking of bacon brought thoughts of the johnnycake his mother made for breakfast each day. It was tasty, but not as delicious as the corn pone she served at midday. Her corn pone was browned on the top and soft and moist in the center. Just thinking about it made John's stomach growl, but it would have to wait.

John chased after the men, relieved when they finally stopped at a small spring to drink. He joined his dad at the water's edge. His father pointed to deer tracks in the soft ground near the spring. "See how even and regular they are," he said. "That's proof they were not disturbed, at least not recently."

"The girls didn't come this way?" John asked.

"Mebbe they did, but if so, the deer came after. Their tracks are fresh, and I don't see any footprints. Do you?"

John could tell that the question was sincere. His dad was actually asking him!

He studied the area, and then shook his head. "No."

His dad put a gentle hand on John's shoulder. "Nor do I," he said. "But keep a lookout. That handkerchief is proof that the girls are trying to help us. Clever girls," he said.

John gulped several hands full of fresh spring water. It dribbled down his chin. Several others joined him. They were all thirsty.

He heard a RUSTLING in the trees. He looked back.

Was someone following them?

No. No one was there. It was probably just an animal. But when he stared into the bushes, he saw something that didn't belong.

What could it be?

He squinted to get a better view. And then he realized what he was seeing.

A white string swayed in the breeze. It didn't belong there. How would a white bit of string end up in this distant forest?

John went to investigate. He plucked the string from the branch. Someone had tied knots in the string. Five knots.

Captain Boone was talking softly to Billy Bush when John approached him with the string in hand. He didn't want to interrupt, but this seemed important.

"Excuse me, Sir," he said and handed Captain Boone the string.

Boone took it. "Jemima!" he said. "I'd know her knots anywhere. Five knots. Five men. They're ahead, but not by much." He rubbed the string between his thumb and forefinger, bowed his head, and rubbed his eyes. "We camp here tonight."

"But Dan'l," Sam Henderson said, "if we got a bit further along . . . ."

"I know. And I want to reach them, too, but we need the light of day. We leave at sunrise tomorrow and catch them by surprise."

John couldn't stop smiling. Not only were they getting close, but he was the one who'd found the clue. No one needed to tell him he'd done a good job. He knew.

The men divided the remaining jerked venison—there was just a bit for each one—and then they settled down for the night.

John's stomach rumbled. It wasn't satisfied, but there was nothing more to eat. Hunting was out of the question. Any gunfire risked alerting the kidnappers. He gulped more spring water to quell his stomach before bedding down on a patch of soft moss.

Captain Boone assigned one of the men to act as

sentry. Sometime well before dawn, the sentry, armed with a tomahawk, sent it flying. "A bear," he said later. "Missed him. Hit the tree instead, but the thud must a scared him off."

John didn't hear either the bear's growl or the tomahawk's thud, but others did. He'd slept well, not only because he was exhausted, but also because he was relieved that he had not only returned with the supplies, but he'd kept up with the men throughout the livelong day and found an important clue.

Maybe the most important one of all.

THE SECOND DAY
Monday, July 15, 1776
Evening

JEMIMA'S STORY

The girls and their kidnappers spent the late afternoon and evening trudging through the wilderness, weaving in and out of cane, climbing over fallen logs, and brushing past bramble bushes. Finally, the men stopped near a fast-flowing stream.

The girls drank their fill and then settled onto a fallen log.

The men were in good spirits. They joked with one another.

Hanging Maw sat down beside Jemima and patted her head. He asked if he could take the combs out of her hair.

Jemima quickly agreed. It would take time to remove the several combs and then replace them. As he pulled the last one away, Jemima's raven-black hair tumbled all the way to her knees. Hanging Maw combed his fingers through her thick locks.

He and the others seemed relaxed now that they had traveled further from Boonesborough. Hanging Maw talked freely with Jemima. His English was excellent. He told her that the men were on their way home from a war council at Chota, the Cherokee capital. Dragging Canoe, one of the young chiefs had invited delegates from the Shawnee, Delaware, Mohawk, Nanticokes, and Ottawa nations. "Some traveled over 70 days to reach Chota, my beloved town, very old," Hanging Maw said. "We wore black paint, a sign of war."

"War?" Jemima asked.

Hanging Maw nodded. "War."

"What did you do there? At Chota?" she asked. It was more than a delay tactic. What war? Was Dragging Canoe planning to attack Boonesborough?

Jemima tried to relax. She tried to appear only mildly interested. Anything to make him tell more. If there was to be war, she had to warn her father. And soon! Before the trouble began.

She pictured her mother bent over the fire stirring the stew, Danny and Jesse tumbling together in the grass, Lavinia and Little Rebecca making mud pies. Were they safe?

She closed her eyes and clenched her fists. She took a cleansing breath and listened as Hanging Maw described how the men had gathered in the village plaza in front of the council house, "where we hold important ceremonies. It has eight sides," Hanging Maw said, "and the posts were painted black and red. War colors."

"What war?" Jemima asked again.

Hanging Maw studied the ground, hesitating. Finally, he looked up and said, "War on the settlements."

"Boonesborough?"

"And others."

"But why? There's a treaty. We bought this land."

Hanging Maw laughed. "No one can own the land any more than they can own the sky or the rivers. The old chiefs tricked the white men. They could not sell something they don't own."

He shook his head. "It was fine for the old men to play at jokes, to let the white men think they now own the land. But the chiefs: they are too old to hunt or fight. The young warriors need the land for hunting. If they cannot provide food to feed a family, they cannot marry." He paused and added, "Dragging Canoe is a powerful speaker. He said to us, 'It is better to die like men than to diminish away by inches.' So, we held a war council. We will meet war parties soon."

He told her that Dragging Canoe would attack the

settlements over the mountains in North Carolina. The Shawnees would attack Kentucky settlements.

"Then why take us?" she asked, pointing to herself and the Callaways. "We did not take your land. We are not hunters."

"We saw you and said, 'why not?' But we didn't know you would be such trouble." He slapped his knee and laughed, which made Jemima smile in return.

"Pretty squaw," Hanging Maw said as he stood up. He patted her on the head. "When we reach the Shawnee villages, you will have a new home."

It was exactly what Jemima expected—and feared. It had happened to other women on the frontier, and now it was happening to her.

The men had treated the girls as they might have treated their own daughters or sisters. Adoption, they called it. They would be adopted into the tribe and live as Shawnee wives and mothers.

In many ways, life among the Shawnee wasn't so different from life at Boonesborough. Settlers and Indians ate the same foods, wore similar clothes, and were at home in the wilderness.

Shawnee ways aren't bad ways.

But I'm not Shawnee.

Jemima wanted to spend her life living with her own tribe: the Boones.

If only her father would come soon.

The Indians no longer seemed worried, and that was a bad sign.

Hanging Maw had been her dad's friend when Daniel Boone was a hunter. But now that he was a settler in Kentucky, he had become an enemy. Settlers cut down trees and built farms. They hunted, not for meat, but for pelts. "They kill too many," Hanging Maw said. Settlers were bad news for wildlife, which meant they were bad news for the Shawnee, the Cherokee, and other tribes. When the animals moved west, the people who depended on them were forced to move, too.

Jemima rubbed her sore foot.

It was the cane's fault.

If she hadn't stepped on that sharp piece of cane, she wouldn't have thought of going for a canoe ride. And if she hadn't gone for the canoe ride, she wouldn't have been kidnapped. Her sore foot had taken her to the wrong place at exactly the wrong time, and now she might have to pay the price for problems she hadn't even caused. Worse yet, she'd brought the Callaways with her.

It wasn't the cane, not really. It was my fault. I suggested the canoe ride. If we never see home again, I'm to blame.

Jemima was so tired she could barely keep moving. She wobbled into the bushes at the side of the path.

Moccasin helped her back onto the trail.

"We stop soon," he said.

Jemima closed her eyes, took a deep breath, and stumbled forward.

An hour later, Hanging Maw led them to a small grove of trees that formed a canopy overhead. He sent Mask to fetch water from a nearby stream, but no one lit a fire. The men may have appeared more relaxed, but Jemima knew they were still—at least a little bit—worried. Otherwise, they would have built a fire and roasted some meat.

The men tied the girls to trees as they had the night before, and then the men sprawled on the ground nearby. They snored and snorted in their sleep.

After she was sure they were asleep, Jemima struggled to reach the knife, which she'd put back into her pocket for safekeeping. If she could reach it and cut the ropes, they could slip away in the dark of night just like her dad had done when he'd been taken.

Freedom. It's so close.

She struggled against the tight ropes. They bit into her skin. She strained against them and stretched her arms until the rope scraped painfully. She felt as if the skin had peeled away. After an hour of trying, she finally relaxed and gave up. It was no use. Her arms were pinned too tightly.

And so, the girls spent a second sleepless night listening to the whine of mosquitoes, the hooting of owls, and the grumbling of their own stomachs. They dozed, but woke when their necks fell forward, their muscles cramped, or the ropes with which they were tied pulled at their arms.

The cooling night breeze brushed Jemima's face, and whenever she woke, she thought of her family at Boonesborough and the people in the other settlements—Harrodsburg, St. Asaph, and Boiling Spring. The tiny settlements were so vulnerable. And if Indians attacked . . . ?

Was her family safe even now? If the men of Boonesborough were searching for her and her friends, who was left to defend the fort? At least her mom was a good shot, almost as good as her dad.

Jemima's face was wet with tears. She not only brought the Callaways into danger, but if something happened to the people at the fort because her Dad was searching for her, she would never forgive herself.

Jemima had never thought deeply about her mom until that night. They worked together every day on household chores, planting the gardens, or tending the children, and when her mother assigned more chores, Jemima grew impatient. Now, though, she'd be happy to do whatever her mother asked of her, if only she could return to the fort and find everyone safe.

Maybe someday she would be as strong and self-reliant as her mother. There was no question that Rebecca Boone was an independent woman. She had to be. After all, she was often the one who had managed the farm and raised the children.

Jemima remembered a time when her Dad finally returned from a long hunt, and no one recognized him. Jemima, her mom, and her brothers and sisters were at a frolic, or dance, at a neighbor's house when he returned. The longhaired stranger, who showed up late, approached Rebecca and asked her to dance.

She refused.

"You need not refuse for you have danced many a time with me," he said with a laugh.

"Daniel!" She recognized his voice if not his bearded face. Rebecca burst into tears and began laughing.

The children rushed forward for hugs, too, and the neighbors gathered round to hear stories of his adventures.

As Jemima leaned against the rough tree, she wondered if she would ever again hear her mother's laugh or see happy tears sparkle on her cheeks.

I'd give anything if I could only go home!

THE THIRD DAY
Tuesday, July 16, 1776
Morning

JOHN'S STORY

Sun sparkling through the treetops woke John at dawn the next morning. He stretched, ate a small bit of jerky, and prepared to push ahead.

Today we'll find the gals.

Oh, how he hoped it was true.

Time was running out. If they didn't find the girls soon, it would be too late. Daniel Boone had said as much the night before.

"What about Callaway and his riders?" Sam Henderson asked.

"We need to get to the girls first," Captain Boone said.

John took that as a warning. If they didn't find them before Callaway, they may end up dead.

John pondered this idea. Would the girls be better off dead than living with the Shawnee? There were plenty of rumors on the frontiers about children kidnapped who claimed to be happier living in an Indian village than living in the settlements. Life with the Indians didn't seem all that terrible.

If John was captured, he'd fit right in. He'd spend his time hunting and fishing, which wasn't so different from the life of a man on the frontier. He wouldn't have to cut lumber and build forts. He'd wear the same togs and eat the same foods as he did now, and he'd never have to go to school or church again, although to be honest, he didn't have to do that in Boonesborough, either.

But Jemima? He knew how she felt about her family. She'd miss them dearly, and they'd miss her.

John felt the tomahawk at his belt. If he had to fight to save her, he'd do it, even at the risk of his own life. He might die, but he'd die a man.

Captain Boone took off racing through the woods, the men trailing behind. No one made a sound. They even tried to calm their breathing.

"We are close," Boone said, and when they arrived at a small stream around ten in the morning, he added, "they crossed a short distance below here."

How could he possibly know?

THE THIRD DAY
Tuesday, July 16, 1776
Morning

JEMIMA'S STORY

The men rose with the sun, eager to begin the next leg of the journey. Hanging Maw nudged Jemima, who had finally fallen into a fitful sleep.

She stared up at the tall Cherokee and thought about what he had told her. He seemed so reasonable as he reported on the meeting at Chota. But how could a reasonable man even think of attacking a fort full of women and children? Would he really lead a war against the settlers? Would he kill innocent children like Lavinia and little Rebecca? She shook her head trying to banish such terrible thoughts.

Had they been wrong to come to Kentucky?

Will Daddy come in time?

Will I have the chance to warn him about the upcom-

ing war?

Can't we find a way to live together in peace?

There were too many questions. Jemima shook her head and rubbed her grumbling stomach. She noticed that the men did likewise.

They must be hungry, too.

They'd been without anything to eat but the jerked buffalo tongue for almost three days.

"We go!" Hanging Maw said, and they lined up and began moving forward.

Around midmorning, they crossed a large creek. The kidnappers kept looking north. Jemima guessed they were looking for the war parties that planned to attack the Kentucky settlements.

When she stared in the same direction, all she saw was endless forest. At first, she thought that was good news. No war party. But maybe it would be better to meet the warriors. The men would be distracted. They'd talk. They'd want to hear the latest news. And that might give the girls a chance to sneak away. Her hands were free, so she didn't need the knife. Even so, she reached into her pocket to reassure herself that it was there.

Fanny shrieked when a small snake slithered across the path.

Bear pulled out his knife and stabbed it. The others gathered round to look.

Jemima fell in beside Fanny as if to comfort her. "Watch for my signal," Jemima whispered. "And run. Tell Betsy."

The men left the snake, still wiggling, in the middle of the trail.

The girls stumbled on. The lack of sleep and food was taking a toll.

"*Yansi*," Hanging Maw said, which meant *buffalo*.

A young bull stood at the edge of the forest path.

"Stay back!" one of the men ordered.

The girls edged away.

Fanny looked to Jemima, searching for the promised signal. Jemima nodded toward Red Paint, who stood guard watching them.

"Not now," she mouthed. Betsy nodded and reached for Fanny's hand. They stood side-by-side as Mask approached the beast.

The buffalo stared at him as he moved closer. It didn't notice that Hanging Maw, Moccasin, and Bear had circled around it and were now blocking an escape.

Jemima heard the snick of an arrow just before the animal fell.

The men wasted no time carving out a tasty portion of the hump.

Jemima hadn't eaten for days but she didn't feel particularly hungry, not anymore. She knew that their willingness to hunt and cook meant they felt safe.

Was no one searching? Had Daddy given up?

Betsy and Fanny stood nearby with shoulders stooped. It was obvious that they were worried, too.

THE THIRD DAY
Tuesday, July 16, 1776
Mid-Day

JOHN'S STORY

There were no signs at all until they found fresh tracks about 200 yards further along. The tracks indicated five men and three girls. Daniel Boone had been right about Jemima's knotted string. Five knots meant five men.

They were close, very close.

Boone led the searchers to the northwest and a short time later found more evidence—bits of cloth, bent twigs, and footprints. And then they found a snake that the Indians had killed. It was still wiggling. The men primed their rifles. John touched his tomahawk with one hand and his knife with the other.

Golly! If only I had a gun. . . .

They moved forward.

A bit further along the trail, they came upon a dead buffalo. Part of its hump had been cut away.

"They'll stop to cook it soon," Boone predicted. He used signals to instruct the men to be silent. The slightest sound would warn the kidnappers and put the girls' lives in grave danger.

He signaled the men to spread out. He sent some of them downstream. Boone headed upstream with John Floyd and William Smith, who served as scout. John followed close behind them.

Their feet made soft splashing sounds in the water. John saw fish scatter. An eagle soared silently overhead.

It was as if the entire world was heeding Boone's instructions.

THE THIRD DAY
Tuesday, July 16, 1776
Mid-Day

JEMIMA'S STORY

The men carried the meat to the nearest stream. After wading across it, they built a cook fire. They prepared the meat, fetched water, and gathered firewood. They were relaxed and carefree.

Bear pulled Betsy's hair as she warmed herself at the fire. She scooped up some coals with a piece of bark and tossed them onto his moccasins.

"Yiii!" He jumped up and down. The coals singed his moccasins, which made the others laugh. They seemed to consider it good fun. No one really disapproved—except, perhaps Bear, who often seemed the butt of their teasing.

Jemima and Fanny sank onto a log about ten feet from the fire.

Hanging Maw approached the girls. He put his hand on one of the combs in Jemima's hair. "Pretty squaw," he said.

Jemima sat absolutely still. She never even looked up at him. None of the men had touched her, other than to help her onto the pony or to shove her along when she veered off the trail. But they were getting closer to the Shawnee Villages. Would she have to marry one of these men? Surely, not Hanging Maw. He was so much older.

Hurry, Daddy. Hurry.

He pointed to his hair. "If you please."

Jemima nodded. His hair was wet. She realized that he wanted her to lock it. After all, he's made a point of noticing her combs. The combs not only kept the hair in place, but they also helped to remove lice. Everyone had lice. Lice didn't care whose head they invaded. Separating the strands of hair with a metal comb and picking out the lice was part of life for most everyone.

Betsy, who was standing by the fire, looked at Jemima and raised an eyebrow.

Fanny shook her head.

But Jemima didn't hesitate. She pulled a comb from her own hair and began using it to separate the strands of Hanging Maw's hair and release the lice and their eggs, called nits. She'd done the same for her sisters at home, and they had done it for her. But this time, it had more than one purpose. Jemima smiled.

Delay, delay, delay.

If removing nits from Hanging Maw's head gave her daddy time to catch up, then it was well worth doing.

Moccasin approached Fanny. She looked to Jemima.

Jemima nodded and mouthed the word, "delay."

Fanny put out her hand to invite Moccasin to take a seat on the log beside her, and she did for him what Jemima was doing for Hanging Maw.

Betsy stood nearby watching.

By the time Jemima and Fanny had completed the task, the fire was roaring.

The men gathered around it and lay their moccasins, tomahawks, and rifles nearby. Hanging Maw and Moccasin began preparing the meat for roasting. The men relaxed. Only Red Paint remained on guard, but he soon propped his rifle against a tree and wandered over to the fire to light his pipe.

Jemima closed her eyes in prayer.

God in Heaven, please help Daddy find us.

Fanny leaned over and whispered in Jemima's ear. "It's too late. No rescue, no escape."

She'd confirmed Jemima's worse fears.

THE THIRD DAY
Tuesday, July 16, 1776
Afternoon

JOHN'S STORY

Suddenly, Smith halted. He waved the men forward. They dropped to their bellies and crawled through the bushes.

John spotted smoke. He smelled burning wood. He followed Boone through the underbrush and peered into the clearing.

John listened. He could just make out the gentle melody of a familiar hymn.

It's one of the girls! It has to be.

Captain Boone gestured for the men to hold their fire until he gave the signal.

John lay hidden in the underbrush. He could see the girls and their Indian captors. He wanted to shout for joy, but he didn't make a sound.

Not a single, solitary sound.

He didn't even breathe.

THE THIRD DAY
Tuesday, July 16, 1776
Afternoon

JEMIMA'S STORY

Jemima hung her head and studied the ground. She was feeling as low as she had ever felt. She barely remembered the long days of being forted or the endless chores.

I thought I wanted freedom then.

But that feeling was nothing like what she felt on this, the third day of captivity. Tears rolled down her cheeks. She reached out for Fanny.

Meanwhile, their captors joked cheerfully with one another as they prepared the feast.

Betsy plunked down on the fallen log between the girls. Their clothes were ragged, their hair tangled, and their faces streaked with sweat and grime. Betsy, who had lost her combs, wore a red bandana around her head to keep her long hair out of her eyes.

Jemima and Fanny laid their heads on Betsy's lap. She ran her fingers through their hair, opening it gently to remove the lice. Betsy cried while she did it, her tears falling into the girls' thick hair. Fanny was crying, too.

Jemima wiped away her own tears. "They'll come," she whispered, but she wasn't sure she really believed it. Neither did Betsy and Fanny. The girls had done everything they could to help the searchers, and there was still no sign of help.

The smell of the wood fire and the roasting buffalo taunted them. The girls should have been hungry. They hadn't eaten since they were captured.

"I don't think I can eat," Betsy said.

"Nor can I," Jemima said.

Fanny lifted her head slightly as if to agree.

Jemima sniffed. "It reminds me of home," she said. "Of Mother tending the fire, corn boiling in the big cast iron pot, and meat roasting on the spit."

"Cuzzy pouring cider into the mugs. . . ," Fanny said.

"The boys calling Father to the table. . . ," Betsy added.

Jemima stared beyond the fire into the nearby bushes.

Such sweet memories.

THE THIRD DAY
Tuesday, July 16, 1776
A Few Minutes Later

JOHN'S STORY

He waited breathlessly in the underbrush. He kept an eye on Daniel Boone, who had his gun on his shoulder, ready to shoot, if necessary. John swung his head around and spotted his father, who squatted behind a nearby pine tree. His rifle was raised and ready, too.

John pulled a leafy branch aside to get a better view. Betsy sat on a log not far from the campfire. She wore a red bandana on her head. The other girls sat beside her with their heads in her lap. Betsy had one hand on each of their heads as if to comfort them.

John felt like yelling "Huzzah!" but he barely dared to breathe. The girls weren't safe, not yet. They were close, so close, but John knew that this might be the most dangerous moment of all.

Quiet was the word, and he intended to obey. The only sounds belonged to nature:

The RUSTLE of leaves as a mouse scurried by.

The KEE-AAH of a hawk in the tree overhead.

The tiny PING of an acorn as it hit the ground.

One of the Indians sat near the girls mending his moccasins. Another added a log to the fire. A third checked the meat roasting on the spit. They didn't seem in a rush to move on, and it was obvious to John that they had no idea anyone was watching.

He recalled Daniel Boone's warning, "Do not fire until I give the signal."

John couldn't fire anyway, but he'd do what he could to get the girls to safety.

THE THIRD DAY
Tuesday, July 16, 1776
A Few Minutes Later

JEMIMA'S STORY

She heard a sound in the bushes. She didn't move. *Could it be?*

Moccasin, who was tending the roast, looked up. He must have heard it too, but he shrugged and returned to the fire.

Jemima sat up.

It had to be!

Oh, she wanted nothing more than to go home. Home to her mother, to her brothers and sisters, to her dad.

She didn't dare make a sound.

She stared into those bushes and saw a slight movement.

She held her breath. Was that her father crawling

toward her?

Yes!

He put a hand to his lips. She wanted to cry out. But she knew better. The only sound was the pounding of her own heart as she watched his every move.

Fanny sat up, too. She watched one of the men turn the meat on the spit. Suddenly, a red spot blossomed on his chest.

Blood!

The sound of a gunshot followed. The man stumbled into the fire. He regained his footing, grabbed his belly, and staggered into the woods.

"That's Daddy!" Jemima cried.

She jumped up and raced toward him.

THE THIRD DAY
Tuesday, July 16, 1776
A Few Minutes Later

JOHN'S STORY

He heard a rustling movement behind him.

Snake?

He shivered.

Golly! Not now.

He lay still. He didn't dare to move lest he alert the kidnappers.

But when he heard a twig snap, he knew it was a man.

As he turned to look, a gun went off.

He saw Jemima run toward her father. Betsy and Fanny sprang after her.

WHIZZ!

A tomahawk sailed through the air. It missed Betsy by a hair.

John gasped. "Stop!" he yelled, knowing that this

time it was the right thing to do.

Captain Boone yelled, too. "Drop! Quick!"

And the girls fell to the ground.

But they popped right back up and raced toward the underbrush where John lay.

He wanted to grab them and lead them to safety, but in the second that he stopped to think, another gunshot rang out.

John couldn't tell who was shooting, but he heard an Indian shout out and saw him run into the woods. The others vanished leaving their moccasins and rifles beside the fire.

John stood up and rushed toward the girls. So did the others.

One of the men raised his rifle to club Betsy.

"Stop!" Boone said, grabbing the man's arm just in time. "For God's sake, don't kill her when we have traveled so far to save her."

The man, a cabin builder who had never seen Betsy before, was horrified at what he had almost done. He tossed down his gun and wept.

John put his hand on the man's shoulder.

"I didn't know," the man said between sobs. "I thought she was one of the Indians."

"She's all right," John said. "And they're gone. Our gals are safe."

THE THIRD DAY
Tuesday, July 16, 1776
Rescue

JEMIMA'S STORY

She ran into her father's arms. "Daddy," she cried and snuggled against his shirt. She smelled the comforting odor of wood smoke and felt his calloused hands tousle her hair.

"You're safe," he whispered, cradling her in his arms.

"Oh, Daddy." It was all she could say. Her heart was full, but she knew if she tried to speak, she'd end up sobbing and babbling incoherently. What she couldn't say out loud, she said in her heart as she hugged her Daddy.

You didn't give up. I knew you wouldn't.

Sam Henderson had his arms around both Betsy and Fanny. The others formed a protective circle around them.

When Jemima looked around, she realized that every one of the Indians had vanished. Their moccasins stood by the fire, their tomahawks and rifles lay on the ground nearby.

Sam Henderson led Betsy and Fanny to the fire.

Daniel Boone followed with Jemima. He wrapped blankets around all three girls and gave them each a mighty hug. "Thank Almighty Providence, boys, for we have the girls safe. Let's all sit down by them now and have a hearty cry."

And they did just that.

THE THIRD DAY
Tuesday, July 16, 1776
Late Afternoon

JOHN'S STORY

When all their tears had been shed, everyone sat around the fire and feasted on roasted buffalo.

John sat beside his dad. His thoughts were jumbled—relief that the search ended well, but just a tiny bit sad that the adventure was over.

Captain Gass put an arm around John's shoulder. "You did well, Son," he said.

John burst into tears. Everyone had done their share of crying that day, so there was no need to be ashamed. He squeezed his dad's hand, the kind of 'thank you' his dad would understand.

Golly, it felt good to be one of the men. I wish—

His dad put his hand on John's shoulder. "Listen," he said.

Everyone had turned to look at Jemima. "A war party is on their way to Boonesborough. That's what Hanging Maw said. They plan to attack other settlements, too."

The men's smiles vanished.

John sat up straighter.

War?

"They are gathering now just a few miles north at the Upper Blue Licks."

Daniel Boone pulled Jemima close. "I've no doubt you heard right, Daughter, and we'll heed the warning. All the more reason to get back to the fort as soon as possible."

John's Dad leaned over and whispered, "So it looks like we might have another battle to fight. It's about time you had a rifle of your own."

It was exactly what John wanted.

For hunting, not for war.

Being a man was not child's play. If it came to war, he would help protect the fort. He knew he could, but he also knew he had a lot to learn, and that his dad and Daniel Boone would be there to teach him.

The men were eager to get back to Boonesborough, but before they left, they made a quick search for the kidnappers.

Three men—William Smith, John Floyd, and Daniel

145

Boone—had fired on the kidnappers. Two had hit their mark.

John joined the others searching the woods for signs. He stopped and listened. He recognized the CHIRPING of birds and SCUTTLING of squirrels leaping from branch to branch. He even heard the distant GROWL of a bear. But he didn't hear anything that sounded like it could be the kidnappers. And then he noticed a bright red splotch on the bark of a tree.

Blood!

Sam Henderson was just ahead. John caught him and said, "I found their trail."

It didn't take Daniel Boone long to confirm the find.

"Will we go after them?" John asked.

Boone shook his head. "No need to track them further. They've run off. We'd best get back to the fort."

They paused long enough to cut as much of the buffalo hump as they could carry.

There was no chance of returning the forty miles to Boonesborough that night. Everyone was exhausted. The group made camp at dusk and roasted more of the meat.

That night no howling wolves or roving bears disturbed anyone's dreams.

THE FOURTH DAY
Wednesday, July 17, 1776
On the Way Home

JEMIMA'S STORY

Jemima fell into a sweet and refreshing sleep. Come morning, her dad said, "Let's go home."

Home. Such a sweet word.

Jemima felt like a new person when they began the trek home. She was joyful, eager to see her mother and her younger brothers and sisters, and ready to do whatever they needed.

She reached out and touched her dad's arm.

There was only one way to show her gratitude. She decided right then and there that she'd stand by him the way he had stood by her.

He can count on me, now and forever.

She studied Betsy and Fanny, hoping she didn't look as dirty as they did, but one look at her own dress disabused her of that notion. Their clothes were rags, their hair unkempt, and their bodies scratched and itchy.

None of it mattered.

They were on the way home.

Sam Henderson insisted on carrying Betsy on his back. Jemima thought that was sweet, but Fanny scoffed. "She can walk as well as we can."

Later that morning, they came upon the white pony. Jemima climbed onto the pony's back. Fanny joined her. So did Betsy, which gave Sam a rest.

John walked beside the horse, and Jemima told him about the last time they had met the pony.

John laughed. "You're a fine rider."

"But they didn't know that," Jemima said, which made John laugh all the harder.

"You're a good friend, John Gass." She hopped off the pony and walked beside John. They slowed down as they spoke, and Fanny rode ahead.

John bowed his head and stared at the ground for a second before looking directly at Jemima.

"I owed you," he said. "You saved my brother. Besides, you're my friend."

Jemima smiled. "You were there when I needed you. It's like my mother says, 'A friend in need is a friend indeed.'"

"*Poor Richard's Almanack*," John said. "My mother

quotes him, too. But I like this one better, 'A true friend is the best possession.'"

Jemima laughed. So did John.

"Friends for life," she said and ran off to catch up with Fanny.

THE FOURTH DAY
Wednesday, July 17, 1776

HOME AT LAST

Colonel Callaway's mounted search team caught up with the girls and their rescuers on the river opposite Boonesborough.

Callaway leaped off his horse to embrace his daughters. There were more tears, more stories.

Flanders rushed to Jemima and took her hand in his. They looked into one another eyes and smiled. Jemima saw the promise there: Someday they would be together, and he would keep her safe.

He lifted Jemima onto his horse, and they rode to the nearest ford together.

Fanny rode behind her father, but Betsy stayed with Sam. They'd wait their turn to take the dugout home.

When the girls and their rescuers finally arrived at

the fort, mothers, brothers, sisters, and friends gathered for a third round of hugs and tears. As Jemima later described it, her mother "both laughed and cried as she always did when she was overjoyed."

And Jemima's foot? By the time she got home, the cane-stab had healed. It didn't take long for her bruises from ropes and brambles to heal either, although Betsy proudly carried the scar of the horse's bite her whole life.

Jemima assured everyone that the kidnappers hadn't hurt them. "The Indians were really kind to us, as much so as they could have been, or as their circumstances permitted."

Many years later, when a niece told Jemima that she would not have allowed Hanging Maw to touch her hair, Jemima responded, "O yes, you would. Every such thing tended to delay their progress, and that was what we studied every art to effect."

The attack on the fort didn't come, not then, but the threat of it forced the men to complete work on the fort to make it more secure.

Three weeks after the girls returned, on August 6, 1776, Betsy married Sam Henderson. Theirs was the first wedding to take place in Kentucky. Betsy wore a simple dress of Irish linen. Sam's best shirt had been tattered and torn during the search, so he borrowed one from a friend. He shaved his face, both sides. Daniel Boone, acting as a local magistrate or judge, performed the ceremony. Instead of cake, wedding guests enjoyed homegrown watermelon.

A week or so later, exciting news reached Boonesborough. The American colonies had declared independence. The colonies were now the United States of America. The delegates to the Second Continental Congress had signed a Declaration of Independence on July 4.

"It happened even before we were taken," Jemima said.

"News is slow to reach us," her mother said.

"Let's hope war is, too," her dad said.

That night, everyone gathered around a huge bonfire for a public reading of the Declaration. When it was done, the men fired their rifles into the air. Jemima smiled at John Gass, who stood proudly with the men, his new rifle by his side.

Daniel Boone brought out his fiddle, and everyone danced by the light of the fire. It was a grand jollification.

The girls were safe, the fort secure, and the country would soon be independent.

AUTHOR'S NOTE

This is a novel based on a real event. Jemima, Fanny, and Betsy told the story of their kidnapping to their children and grandchildren. Newspapers reported it. Daniel Boone himself included it in his autobiography. Here's what he had to say:

> "On the fourteenth day of July 1776, two of Col. Callaway's daughters, and one of mine, were taken prisoners near the fort. I immediately pursued the Indians, with only eight men, and on the sixteenth overtook them, killed two of their party, and recovered the girls."

The account above is from The Adventures of Col. Daniel Boone: Containing a Narrative of the Wars of Kentucky. It is part of a book written by John Filson, The Discovery and Settlement of Kentucky. It was published in 1784 and soon became a best-seller. Filson's book helped make Daniel Boone a hero. Filson spent several weeks with Daniel Boone listening to his stories. Filson claimed that Boone wrote his own autobiography, but that's probably not true. Many experts believe that Filson actually did the writing based on the stories Boone told him.

I have tried to stay true to the story. We cannot know, of course, what the girls or the kidnappers or the searchers were thinking at any particular time, but we can imagine it based on their actions. Throughout the kidnapping, Jemima remained focused on leaving clues and delaying the journey. Daniel Boone was intent on finding the girls, and the kidnappers did everything in their power to get back to their villages.

And what about John Gass? History records that he did swim the river to retrieve the canoe. He began the search and returned to Boonesborough for supplies. Did he actually continue the search with Daniel Boone? Some historians say that he was sent back to the fort after he returned with supplies. But I imagined John as someone who wanted to continue searching until his friend was found. He seemed to be that kind of boy.

Fights between frontier settlers and various American Indian tribes are a fact of history. These are often sad stories. Entire communities were destroyed on both sides. It's tempting to pretend that this did not happen. But it did. Learning about our history, understanding not only what happened but why, helps us to make better decisions in the future.

History is not just about the past. It can lead us into a better future.

GLOSSARY

Some words you may not know:

Alarm—to sound a warning

breechclout—a single piece of cloth wrapped around the hips; also called a loincloth

buffalo trace—a trail made by a herd of buffalo

cane—a tall bamboo-like grass

dugout—a kind of canoe made by hollowing out a log

ford—a place where a river is shallow so that it is possible to wade across

frontiersman—a person who is skilled at living on unsettled land

gut-foundered—hungry (18th century)

jollification—celebration or merrymaking (18th-century usage)

palisade—a tall fence made of pointed logs designed to defend a fort

pantaloons—tight-fitting men's trousers

pinion—to bind a person's arms and hands so that they cannot use them

prime—to put powder in a rifle so it is ready to fire

savvy—a way of saying, "I understand" (18th-century usage)

scalp lock—a long lock of hair left on a shaved head

siege—a blockade designed to keep people from getting the supplies they need and forcing their surrender

stockade—a barrier made with posts and stakes for defense

togs—clothing (18th-century usage)

venison—meat from a deer

A FEW ADDITIONAL Q & A'S

Q **What happened to Hanging Maw and the other kidnappers?**

A Two years after the kidnapping, Daniel Boone learned that the two Indians who had been wounded during the rescue died of their wounds. One of the dead men was the son of Chief Blackfish. In 1778, Chief Blackfish captured Daniel Boone during a salt-making expedition. Blackfish adopted Daniel Boone to replace the son he had lost. Later, of course, Boone escaped and returned to Boonesborough.

Hanging Maw, whose Cherokee name was Scolacutta (Usk-wa'li-gu'ta in the Cherokee language) returned to the Cherokee towns in the southern mountains. As chief of the Cherokee Nation from 1780-1792, he urged peace with the settlers. When he died in 1796, *The New York Herald* described him as "a man distinguished by his love of peace." Why did he capture the girls? The younger Shawnee braves probably initiated the kidnapping. Hanging Maw may have felt honor-bound to help his brothers.

Q What were the complaints that the Shawnee and Cherokee had concerning the settlers?

A The tribes wanted to protect their land from settlers. Settlers changed the land itself: cutting down trees, plowing and planting the land, building cabins, and herding livestock. These changes threatened the tribes' traditional way of life. The Shawnees complained that the settlers were "coming in the middle of us like crazy people and want to shove us off our land entirely."

Without land for hunting, it would be extremely difficult for the tribes to survive. They had established large villages in the Ohio River Valley where the women farmed the land, but the people still depended on hunting as their major food source.

White hunters, many Shawnees complained, did not behave like native hunters. Some white hunters killed for the thrill of it; others killed for the furs, leaving the meat behind to rot. Native hunters, on the other hand, felt a kinship with the animals. They treated them with respect, offered prayers, and gave thanks to the animals they killed. They also used every part of the animal when possible to support their families. As more and more white settlers arrived, it became increasingly difficult for the Indians to maintain their way of life. The threat was serious enough to warrant raids and attacks.

Q Did the girls talk about the kidnapping?

A Yes. As they grew up, married, and had children of their own, Jemima, Fanny, and Betsy often told the story of the three days they spent as captives. All three reported that they were treated well—under the circumstances. Jemima Boone, like her father, never portrayed the Indians as cruel or abusive. She insisted that Hanging Maw and the others treated them gently. They may have threatened them, but they never raised a hand to harm them.

Q Did the girls stay in Boonesborough?

A Eventually, Jemima married Flanders Callaway. Jemima and Flanders moved to Missouri when Jemima's parents relocated there. They had eleven children and many grandchildren. Jemima stayed close to her father throughout her life. After the kidnapping, she vowed never to stray far from his side again. She was with him when he died on September 26, 1820, at age 85. Jemima died 9 years later at age 67.

Fanny married John Holder. They moved to Holder's Station, across the river from Boonesborough. They raised 8 children in Kentucky. They were living there when Kentucky became a state on June 1, 1792.

Betsy and Sam Henderson moved back to North Carolina in the fall of 1777. They had ten or eleven children, and eventually moved to Tennessee.

Q What about John Gass?

A John and his family remained in Boonesborough for several years. He defended the fort during various attacks. Later in life, he wrote many letters about life in Boonesborough, the kidnapping, and the sieges on the fort to a historian collecting materials about Boonesborough. His letters helped to create the historical record.

Q What happened to Boonesborough?

A The fort was not attacked during the search for the girls. However, a band of warriors had burned an outlying cabin belonging to Nathaniel Hart and ruined his young apple trees. It served as a warning. The settlers took more precautions, keeping women and children safe within the fort, completing the palisade, and assigning armed men to guard the crops and the livestock.

Although there were no major attacks on Boonesborough in 1776, other Kentucky settlements weren't so lucky. The constant threats led many people to move back East. At times, especially during the Revolutionary War, more people were traveling East on the Wilderness Road (originally called Boone's Trace) than there were traveling West.

In 1777, several small skirmishes took place at Boonesborough. In May of that year, a war party of about 200 men attacked the fort. The attack lasted for two days before the Indians retreated. There was another attack in June. No one at the fort was killed, but the settlers lost several cattle. There is no record of Shawnee losses.

In January of 1778, Daniel Boone led a party of thirty men to a saltlick. They spent days boiling down the water to make salt, which they needed in order to preserve meat. A large group of Shawnee warriors kidnapped most of the men, including Daniel Boone. By May, Rebecca Boone assumed that her husband was dead. She and her children returned to North Carolina. Only

Jemima and Flanders remained in Boonesborough with the other settlers to await the men's return.

Daniel Boone escaped and warned the settlers at Boonesborough that an attack was likely. It happened on September 7, 1778. A party of 400 Shawnee warriors and 40 French Canadians attacked the fort. This was in the midst of the Revolutionary War, at a time when the British had recruited many Native tribes to join them with the promise to drive the settlers out and return the land to the tribes.

Boone attempted to talk peace, but the siege lasted for eleven days.

Finally, the Shawnees and their allies gave up. They returned to their villages, having lost many of their number.

Boonesborough suffered, too, but not as badly as the attacking force. Two Boonesborough men and many cattle were killed during the siege. The men and women at the fort fought hard. Sixty men, both black and white, joined the battle to protect the settlement against the huge force. (The Callaways and a few other families owned slaves. The Boones did not.)

The women who lived at the fort not only cared for the wounded and made bullets, but they also loaded the rifles and even shot them. As one eyewitness said, "the ladies themselves repeatedly fired at the Indians." Everyone did his or her part.

In November 1778, Daniel Boone, Jemima, and Flanders returned to North Carolina. It was nearly a year later that they made it back to Boonesborough with the entire family and several additional settlers. They did not remain there long. It was too crowded for Daniel Boone, who was always seeking "elbow room." He moved his family to a site about six miles northwest of Boonesborough, where he founded a new settlement, Boone's Station. Eventually, the family moved further west to Missouri.

They were not alone in moving west. By 1810, only a handful of people remained in Boonesborough. Soon after, the settlement was deserted. Today, a replica of the fort stands on the ground of Fort Boonesborough State Park in present-day Richmond, Kentucky.

Q Did the Revolutionary War make an impact on the frontier?

A The Revolutionary War had begun even before the girls were kidnapped. In the original thirteen states, George Washington's Continental Army and local Patriot militias (volunteer soldiers) fought British troops.

The war was different on the Western frontier. Indian warriors waged surprise attacks on small outposts like Boonesborough. Many British leaders encouraged and supported these attacks. Sometimes American Indians fought with British troops. But more often, Native Americans were waging their own war of independence. They wanted to reclaim their hunting grounds so that they could be free to live as their ancestors had for hundreds of years.

TIMELINE

Oct. 22, 1734   Daniel Boone is born in Exeter township in Pennsylvania.

Aug. 15, 1756   Daniel marries Rebecca Bryan. They settle in North Carolina.

May 3, 1757   First child, James, is born.

Nov. 2, 1760   Daniel Boone first visits Kentucky on a long hunt.

Oct. 4, 1762   Jemima is born.

1769   Daniel Boone goes to Kentucky on a long hunt; he's captured by Shawnees and escapes.

1773   Boone family attempts a move to Kentucky; James is killed in Indian attack.

March 1775   Boone leads a group of frontiersmen assigned to cut the road to Kentucky. The rough road was initially called Boone's Trace, and later renamed the Wilderness Trail.

April 1775   Boone founds Boonesborough; and brings family to Boonesborough. The first shots of the Revolutionary War are fired at Lexington and Concord, Massachusetts.

September 1775   Boone family arrives at Boonesborough.

July 4, 1776   Congress adopts the "Declaration of Independence."

July 14, 1776   Jemima Boone, and Fanny and Elizabeth Callaway are kidnapped.

July 16, 1776   Daniel Boone finds the girls and brings them home.

Aug.1776   News of the "Declaration of Independence" reaches Boonesborough.

Aug. 6, 1776   Betsy Callaway marries Sam Henderson; Daniel Boone performs the ceremony.

Spring 1777   Jemima Boone marries Flanders Callaway.

1778   Boone is captured by Shawnees in February; he escapes in June; Shawnees attack Boonesborough from Sept. 7-18.

1779   Daniel Boone moves further west and founds Boone's Station where he lives with Rebecca Boone and their children, including Jemima and   Flanders Callaway.

1781   Daniel Boone is elected to the Virginia Legislature.

Oct. 19, 1781   The British surrender at Yorktown; the Revolutionary War is over. Skirmishes continue on the frontier.

June 1, 1792   Kentucky becomes the 15th state in the Union.

1799   The Boone family moves to Missouri.

Sept. 26, 1820   Daniel Boone dies; he's buried near Jemima's farm.

1829   Jemima Boone Callaway dies in Missouri.

SOURCES CONSULTED

Abbott, John S. C. *Daniel Boone: Pioneer of Kentucky*. New York: Dodd, Mead and Company, 1872.

Arnow, Harriette Simpson. *Seedtime on the Cumberland*. Lexington: University of Kentucky Press, 1984.

Aron, Stephen. "Daniel Boone and the Struggle for Independence on the Revolutionary Frontier," in *The Human Tradition in the American Revolution*, ed. by Nancy L. Rhoden and Ian K. Steel, Wilmington, DE: SR Books, 2000; 139-157.

Bakeless, John. *Daniel Boone*. Harrisburg, Penn.: Stackpole Company, 1965; 124-140.

"Bison Bellows: Bison East of The Mississippi," accessed 06/15/21 online at: https://www.nps.gov/articles/bison-bellows-9-16-16.htm

Brown, Meredith Mason. Frontiersman: Daniel Boone and the Making of America. Baton Rouge: Louisiana State University, 2008.

Bruce, H. Addington. *Daniel Boone and the Wilderness Trail*. New York: Macmillan, 1951.

Callaway, Colin G. *The Shawnees and the War for America*. New York: Viking, 2007.

- - - *TheAmerican Revolution in Indian Country: Crisis and Diversity in Native American Communities*. New York: Cambridge University Press, 1995.

Caperton, Mrs. James and Katherine Phelps. "A Partial List of

Those at Fort Boonesborough," *Register of Kentucky State Historical Society*, Vol. 23, No. 68 (May 1925); 142-161.

Clark, Thomas. *Kentucky: A Students' Guide to Localized History*. New York: Teachers College Press, 1965.

Collins, Lewis. *Historical Sketches of Kentucky: Embracing Its History, Antiquities,and Natural Curiosities, Geographical, Statistical, and Geological Descriptions; with Anecdotes of Pioneer Life . . . .* Maysville, KY, 1848.(Reprint edition Arno Press & The New York Times, 1971).

Draper, Lyman C. *The Life of Daniel Boone*, edited by Ted Franklin Belue. Mechanicsburg, PA: Stackpole, 1998.

Eckert, Allan W. *The Frontiersmen: A Narrative*. Boston: Little, Brown and Company, 1967.

Enoch, Harry G. and Anne Crabb. *Women at Fort Boonesborough 1775-1784*. Fort Boonesborough Foundation, 2014.

Eslinger, Ellen, ed. *Running Mad for Kentucky: Frontier Travel Accounts*. Lexington: University of Kentucky Press, 2004.

Every, Dale Van. *Men of the Western Waters*. Boston: Houghton Mifflin, 1956.

Daniel Boone: *The Life and Legend of an American Pioneer*. New York: Henry Holt and Company, 1992; 130-140.

Filson, John. *The Adventures of Col. Daniel Boone Containing a Narrative of the Wars of Kentucky From the Discovery and Settlement of Kentucky* (originally published in 1784, now available at Project Gutenberg or in facsimile – Ann Arbor, Mich: University Microfilms, 1966).

Fountain, William, Ph.D., Extension Professor, Univ. of Ky Dept. of Horticulture. Comments via email concerning wildflowers and plants along the Kentucky River.

Hammon, Neal O., Ed. *My Father, Daniel Boone: The Draper Interviews with Nathan Boone*. Lexington: University Press of Kentucky, 1999.

Harrison, Lowell Hayes. *A New History of Kentucky*. University of Kentucky Press, 1997.

Hurt, R. Douglas. *Nathan Boone and the American Frontier*. Columbia, Mo.: University of Missouri Press, 1998.

Kincaid, Robert L. *The Wilderness Road*. Indianapolis, Ind.: Bobbs-Merrill 1947.

Lofaro, Michael A. *Daniel Boone: An American Life*. Lexington: University of Kentucky Press, 2003; 68-75.

Moore, Arthur K. *The Frontier Mind*. New York: McGraw-Hill, 1957.

Morgan, Robert. *Boone: A Biography*. Chapel Hill, N.C.: Algonquin Books of Chapel Hill, 2007; 202-213.

Parmenter, Jon W. "Dragging Canoe (Tsi'yu-gûnsi'ni): Chickamauga Cherokee Patriot," in *The Human Tradition in the American Revolution*, ed. by Nancy L. Rhoden and Ian K. Steel, Wilmington, DE: SR Books, 2000; 117-137.

Perkins, James H. *Annals of the West: Embracing a Concise Account of Principal Events, Which Have Occurred in the Western States and Territories, from the Discovery of the Mississippi Valley to the Year Eighteen Hundred and Fifty*. St. Louis: James R. Albach, 1851.

Rutkow, Eric. American Canopy: Trees, Forests, and the Making of a Nation. New York: Scribner's, 2012.

Sale, Richard T. "Daniel Boone: Beyond the Settlements," *Into the Wilderness*. Washington, D.C.: National Geographic Society, 1983; 64-86.

Seelye, James, Jr., and Steven Alden Littleton. *Voices of the American Indians; Vol. 1*. ABC-CLIO, 2012.

Thornton, Russell. *The Cherokees: A Population History*. Lincoln: University of Nebraska Press, 1990.

White, Stewart Edward. *Daniel Boone: Wilderness Scout: The Life Story and True Adventures of the Great Hunter Long Knife who first blazed the Wilderness Trail through the Indians Country to Kentucky*, New York: Doubleday, 1922; 148-153.

Websites:

Kentucky State Parks: Fort Boonesborough http://parks.ky.gov/parks/recreationparks/Fort-Boonesborough/default.aspx

National Park Service: Cumberland Gap National Park http://www.nps.gov/cuga/index.htm

Boone Historical Sites: http://www.Boonesociety.org/historical_links/historical_sites.htm

Information on cane courtesy of David Taylor, a botanist with the US Forestry Service in Kentucky contacted by phone (859-745-3167) on 10/27/2014.

ACKNOWLEDGMENTS

This book would not exist without the men and women who collected, preserved, and retold the story of what happened in Kentucky in 1776. I have tried to stay true to their accounts, at least as true as a novel can be. Their names are listed in the *Sources Consulted*. Thanks also to Amanda Sears, Madison Country [Kentucky] Horticultural Agent, Beverly James, Preserve Director at the Floracliff Nature Sanctuary [Lexington, Kentucky], and Colin G. Calloway, Professor of History and Native American Studies at Dartmouth College. They responded to specific questions with expert answers.

I am grateful to the team at Chicken Scratch Books, especially editor Kiri Jorgensen, who embraced Jemima's story with enthusiasm and provided excellent editorial guidance, and also to Crystal Brinkerhoff, who guided this book into the hands of readers.

My Fargo, North Dakota, critique group continues to provide support, encouragement, and wise advice. Kristy Olsgaard, Linda Sand, June Dordal, Tory Christy, Michelle Lundstrom, and Elise Parsley critiqued this book when it was in its infancy. Cindy Mason, Missy Jackson, Terrie Enlow, and Deirdre Prischmann critiqued later versions.

As always, I rely on the support and encouragement of family. First reader, Greta Raum, provided insightful comments from a young person's perspective. My son Matt, who loves history as much as I do, urged me to include John's story in this novel. My husband, Richard, has joined me on many adventures. For this novel, we traveled to Fort Boonesborough State Park in Richmond, Kentucky. His patience, encouragement, and love make every project possible

ABOUT THE AUTHOR

When Elizabeth Raum was in 3rd grade, her teacher predicted that she would become a writer. It seemed impossible. Now, 150 books later, Elizabeth admits that Mrs. Brown could see into the future. Of course, it didn't happen right away. Elizabeth became a teacher and then a librarian before turning to writing fulltime. She's written biographies, nonfiction books on many topics, picture books, and several middle-grade historical novels. Her latest novel, *Storm Warning*, is a fictional account of the 1997 Red River Valley flood in North Dakota and Minnesota. She's lived in seven different states and currently splits her time between North Dakota and Tennessee, enjoying the beauty of both prairie and mountains. She's delighted to be working with Chicken Scratch Books. Be sure to visit her website: www.elizabethraumbooks.com

Chicken Scratch Reading School

A Kidnapping In Kentucky 1776

Online Novel Study Courses

www.chickenscratchbooks.com/courses

Join us at Chicken Scratch Reading School for your choice of 2 different online Novel Study Courses for *A Kidnapping In Kentucky 1776*. Created by certified teachers with extensive curriculum design experience, these offerings are 4 or 6-week courses of study for 5th- 8th grade students. They include reading study focus, interviews, quizzes, vocabulary work, thematic and character analysis, a written essay, and culmination project. The courses include a mix of online and on-paper work, highlighted by instructional videos from the author, Elizabeth Raum, and publisher Kiri Jorgensen.

We creates online novel study courses for every book we publish.

Our goal is to teach readers to love new traditional literature.

At Chicken Scratch Books,
Traditional Literature is all we do.

We Fill the Gap

Mainstream Publishers

Religious Publishers

Mainstream and Religious
Children's Book Publishers
used to run side-by-side.

Now they've split